BREAK IN

GW00793037

Mike Parker has worked as a teacher since 1990. He has published many short stories and poems in magazines throughout the world. Each year he writes and performs a one-man show. He currently lives in the west of England with his wife Linda and their four children.

BREAK-IN

BREAK-IN

Mike Parker

WOLFHOUND PRESS

Published in 2002 by
Wolfhound Press
An imprint of Merlin Publishing
16 Upper Pembroke Street
Dublin 2
Ireland
Tel: + 353 1 6764373
Fax: + 353 1 6764368
E-mail: publishing@merlin.ie
www.merlin-publishing.com

Text copyright © 2002 Mike Parker
Design and Layout © 2002 Merlin Publishing
Cover photograph © Ghislain and Marie David de Lossy/Getty
Images

British Library Cataloguing in Publication Data
A catalogue record for this book is available from the
British Library

ISBN 0-86327-898-1

5 4 3 2 1

Typeset by Gough Typesetting Services
Cover design by Pierce Design
Printed by Cox & Wyman Ltd

To Linda, Felix, Rosa, Bertie and Nellie

One

The figure in the back garden smiled to himself. He wasn't just protected by the darkness, he was safe because of his superior knowledge. He scanned the house: its lights were turned off, the doors were locked and the residents were out. No alarm either, no security at all – except the gravel. He smiled again. He'd seen that advice programme on morning TV as well. Put a gravel path round the house, under the windows, some know-all had suggested. It puts off burglars because they can be heard. *Can't be heard if there's no one in to hear,* he thought.

He motioned to the three lads waiting behind the buddleia bush to come forward.

'Any problems?' asked a half-anxious voice. Gavin, nervous as usual, despite his imposing bulk. Not just cautious, downright nervous.

'A few old tricks,' whispered Mark. 'They've put cactuses in the window-boxes – that sort of stuff.'

'Hey, we saw that programme ...' interrupted another voice.

'Shut up, Trev. Not so loud.' Mark was surveying the back door, his head completely still, only his intense blue eyes flicking back and forth. They all fell silent. You had to respect the one who made sure you never got caught. And they never had.

'How do we get in?' asked Gavin. Always asking, always asking.

'Simple back-door job. None of that fancy reinforced glass.' Mark crept forward, avoiding the gravel, and knelt by the back door. A very faint light from some electrical appliance shimmered in the kitchen beyond. He hummed. They'd even left the key in. Some people did that, in the mistaken belief that it stopped you fitting another key in and kept the door safe. 'Ricky, come here. It's got a cat-flap.'

Ricky crept forward. He was long and thin, with a pale face and dark eyes; he was seventeen, but he looked younger. He waited while Gavin broke the plastic lock on the cat-flap by brute force without making a sound. Ricky couldn't believe the casualness of the householders. Didn't they think they had anything worth stealing?

He scraped over to the flap and poked in his long, skinny arm, stretching up towards the key lodged in the lock. He couldn't quite reach. He twisted round and snaked out his arm again, just touching the cold eye of the key.

'Can't turn it, I don't think....' he hissed.

Mark reviewed his watch: if it took longer than five minutes to get in, he'd call it off. He listened to the distant grunting of traffic on the dual carriageway and the flushing of a bog three doors down. The autumn chill of the garden kept him alert.

Ricky swivelled again and arched his back. 'Got it ...' The key dropped to the kitchen floor with a ring that sounded as loud as a ship's bell. Ricky scrabbled on the floor, his hand fumbling blindly for the dropped key. 'Got it,' he repeated, and withdrew his hand, holding up an old-fashioned latchkey.

Mark snatched it and fitted it in the lock, hoping that there were no bolts, or that they hadn't been drawn. He knew Gavin would be bursting for the bog, after the adrenaline rush of climbing the back wall and squirming across the gardens. He knew Trev would want to go through the lady's wardrobe and take some clothes. Ricky, he guessed, was already satisfied: his weird long arms had done the trick yet again.

The key clicked and the door moved. No bolts. Mark crawled in first, and the others wriggled after him. They knew the occupants were out for the night. The couple had departed in a taxi, in their clubbing gear, half an hour earlier. There was a slim chance they might return, but that was part of the deal, part of the pleasure.

Mark wriggled to the lounge and over to the window. He sat up and drew the curtains before standing up and watching the others arrive. He was always watching, Mark; like a predator before the kill, with those eyes and that stillness.

'Gavin, if you've forgotten the back door, I'll have you,' he hissed.

'Gav, forget? No chance. He's probably double-bolted it,' laughed Trev. 'He's that scared.' Trevor being protective as usual: crafty, careful Trevor.

'Like the owners should've,' said Ricky quietly, flexing his arm.

'Pull the blinds in the kitchen, Trev,' ordered Mark. 'Then we'll have this standard lamp on.' He looked round proudly, as if he owned the house; as if he'd bought it, restored it, decorated it, furnished it and made a home of it. It was his for the time being.

Trev returned from the kitchen. 'Done.' Mark relied on Trev to keep calm. Trev had a way of creeping about places, without noise or fuss.

'Now,' said Mark, 'most people get in, whip something and get out quick as poss. Not us.' They knew the speech. 'We're not unemployed ... we're otherwise employed. Let's see what's on offer. Turn the box on, Gavin. It's the live football tonight.'

9

They left Gavin in the front room and went back to the kitchen. Mark turned on an up-light, rather than the fluorescent strip. Good thick blinds, he noticed, nice kitchen; plenty of worktops.

Ricky was inspecting the fridge. 'Excellent,' he said admiringly. 'Bacon, eggs, black pud ... some sausages, too. People after our own hearts.'

'Get cracking,' said Mark.

Trev lit the gas stove and sorted out a frying-pan and two saucepans. He ignited the grill and found the bread bin, humming to himself. Ricky brought over oil and margarine and a couple of tins of baked beans. Mark did the crockery and cutlery. They knew the routine.

'I knew Home Ec would come in handy,' laughed Trev, glancing at Mark to assess his mood.

'Don't go upstairs, Trev,' ordered Mark, catching the glance. 'Except for the bog. If you do....'

'Any beer?' asked Gav, appearing in the doorway. 'Fifteen minutes till kick-off. You don't think they might come back for the match, do you?'

'Maybe,' replied Mark. He left the room, and they heard him fiddling with the front door; after a moment he was back. 'I've dropped the catch and put on the chain. It'll give us enough time, if they come back.' He went to the lounge and settled down, waiting for his chefs to serve up.

They were quick and expert. Within fifteen minutes, the four of them were settled in front of the telly, a full plate on each lap and a tower of buttered bread in the middle. The house smelt of fry-ups; that warm café smell of fat and meat and egg. Trev had been upstairs to the bog, but he'd heeded Mark's advice – he knew Mark would be timing him; Gav had gone first thing, as Mark

10

had guessed he would, leaving the place in a state. The commentator added a different excitement to their already buzzing nervous systems, and yet, this was the life: this was luxury, this was almost home. Mark held up his can of beer.

'The Breakfast Boys,' he toasted.

Geoff Lindenfield was a big man, at work and at home. He rose early and worked late at his building company. It was a smallish company, but solid and hard as a brick. He still laboured on the sites, between doing the account books and setting up orders.

He didn't want his son Gavin working for him. Final. His son had to make it elsewhere first, before Geoff gave him a chance in the company. It didn't look likely, the way Gavin hung around on the dole with his loser friends – that Mark article and that long streak of nothing Ricky and that oily git Trevor, the junior ladies' man. And Gavin had that look on his face all the time – that look of contempt. *Give me that look,* thought Geoff, *I'll give you something back.* But he felt ... he suddenly realised he felt jealous of his son. *Why? Maybe Gavin reminds me of someone. . . .*

Gavin didn't want to work for his dad; he didn't want to work, full stop. *I don't have to do that,* he'd thought a thousand times; *why should I become just a version of him?* Besides, his dad made him jumpy. And work seemed like an endless, funless, pointless routine that went round and round like one of his dad's cement mixers, slopping out mixture that somebody shovelled up while the next lot went in to be minced. Round and round. Why should he be minced up in the boredom of it all?

'Spurs won three to one last night,' Geoff said to Gavin over breakfast – a fry-up Gavin didn't want after the night before. 'But you wouldn't've seen it. Out again – every night, like a cat.' Geoff called out towards the kitchen, 'Our son's a cat, Mags. Sits on a bleedin' wall at night, singin' – that's why he's never in after dark. Either that or he's a bloody vampire.'

Gavin kept quiet and looked at Geoff's bunched hands and wooden shoulders. He was taller than his dad, but Geoff had the build of a piece of heavy furniture, and scary blue eyes that ought to have been attractive but weren't. His dad had the look of someone forever stuck at the traffic lights and bloody angry about it.

Say nothing, thought Gavin. *I saw the game all right, but I'm saying nothing.*

'What's that look for? What were you doing?' barked Geoff, frustrated by his son's lifelessness. 'Nothing, I expect. Not even drinking.' To Mags: 'Not even drunk.' He snorted. 'Couldn't afford it. I'd give you the money if I thought you'd waste it properly ....'

Gavin wondered how strong his father really was.

'... If it isn't bloody American, your age don't want to know. You'd buy sewage if it came from the US. Well, this ain't America – it's here.' Geoff sipped his coffee. 'Bloody America. Why do they have those bloody great long shorts on for basketball, eh? Got cold legs, have they?' Geoff watched a lot of sport. 'And that ...'

That organ drives me mad in the background, Gavin completed in his head.

'... in the background,' finished Geoff.

If he loves work so much, why's he take it out on me, every day before he goes, thought Gavin, *every day, every*

12

day. When I'm up he takes it out on me; when I'm asleep he
wakes me up to take it out. He's not happy.... One day, I'll
smack him one. I'll slap him about. I'll ...

'What's that look on your face?' snapped Geoff, who
was used to working with men with short tempers and
knew the signs. 'You can wipe that off, for starters.'

'What look?' whispered Gavin, too late.

'That look. The one that's still there.' Geoff started to
rise. 'Having thoughts, then? Hey, Mags, it does think
after all.' *I can sort this out now, once and for all.*

Gavin felt his fears return. His dad looked dark and
deadly, and his tight grin showed the gap where he'd lost
a tooth in a fight years back.

'Getting big, eh?' muttered Geoff. 'Big man's left school
and he's a real man on the dole, all of a sudden.'

Gavin wondered why his mum wasn't coming out of
the kitchen to smooth things over. He realised, suddenly,
that she was fed up with him too. But surely she didn't
think Dad going ballistic was going to do him some good,
did she? Gavin wanted to retreat, but he couldn't; and he
knew 'that look' was still on his face, he had no control
over it. He knew he was looking bitter and angry and
resentful, full of hatred and contempt.

'I've handled some big blokes before now....' Geoff
was saying, but Gavin barely heard. All he saw was his
dad advancing, a huge shirt and boots and scarred fists.
He couldn't believe it: his dad was going to belt him one.
His dad was taking him on like some drunk in a pub.

'Bigger than you....' His dad seemed to be talking to
himself about some other enemy.

Then it flashed from nowhere: a punch. A deep, hard
punch on the chin; not the quick snapping punch of one
of Gavin's friends, but a crunching rock of a hit. It

13

slammed into the bone of Gavin's jaw, and the sheer body weight behind it threw him against the wall.

Geoff followed up, but with less force, because the first blow had shown him he was still much stronger than his son. Gavin's legs gave a little, but he didn't go down.

It was amazing: he didn't go down. The punch had been hard, really hard; but not *that* hard, not as hard as a train or a wall hitting you. Dazed as he was, Gavin felt a weird pride at being upright still.

Geoff backed off in embarrassment, and Gavin slid along the wall towards the door. He knew Geoff wasn't going to chase after him. He saw his mum coming out from the kitchen; but her eyes were on her husband, as if she admired him.

'You'll be old one day,' Gavin found himself shouting. 'Old and weak. And I'll come back and I'll beat the living daylights out of you. Old and weak and you won't be able to defend yourself and you'll be scared of me....' And he ran for the front door. Before he darted out, he shouted, 'And America's much better than this pile of crap you call a town, and the companies over there make more money in a day than you make in a year!'

Ricky liked evening in the park. He always arrived early, before the others, to sit and look around at the odd people who pottered about with their dogs and sticks. The shrubs and bushes gave off a strong scent of autumn and he enjoyed being a little bit cold. Even in summer, he felt the changes in temperature, because of his thinness. Like an underfed dog, his mother said – although she constantly worried about her figure, which was still slim. Her friends said she was lucky to have had a kid while she was young; got it out the way early, they said. Not that Ricky didn't eat. He was a waste-disposal unit in jeans. Lots of brown cells, he'd read once. People with brown cells stayed skinny. It was quite a feat, being as thin as him. His uncles – he seemed to have hundreds of them – said he should keep his hair short, otherwise he wouldn't have the strength to keep his head upright. His thinness was everyone's joke, except when Mark needed it to get into houses.

Being a Breakfast Boy suited him down to the ground – great job. Only work a few nights a week, and as much food as you could eat.

'I'm not a thief,' he muttered to himself. 'I'm a bloody chef.'

Last night, they'd even done the washing-up for that couple and cleaned the worktops (which were filthy; the couple obviously worked too much to clean). What was a bit of grub and the use of the house for the night? Nothing. In fact, them being there had probably stopped the house being burgled by greedier raiders. It was practically a service the Breakfast Boys provided.

Trev arrived first. Walking lazily, slowly. Did Trev worry about anything?

'Did we get in?' asked Ricky straightaway, as soon as Trevor was within earshot.

'Yep,' said Trevor, who read the local papers. 'Small mention – something like "Grub Gang Raids Another Fridge". They still don't understand it. I don't think they believe the people. I mean, who breaks into a house and cooks a fried meal and then leaves?' He smiled. 'Funny idea. But then, Mark's . . .'

Trevor stroked his sideburns, which made him look older; older than any of them, in fact. Which he was, of course – the casual confidence he'd always had came not just from his looks, but from being one of the oldest lads in their year at school. Ricky'd hoped it would all even itself out when they got to sixteen; but now Trev had turned eighteen, and the rest of them were still seventeen – and school felt like it had been years ago – and Trev still seemed older.

'I can't believe we only left school last July,' said Ricky.

'Why?'

'Dunno. Just seems like ages.'

'Might as well be,' said Trev, and sat down. He wasn't too fussed about time. He mostly felt like he was living in some timeless bubble from a sci-fi story.

They stared over the park, looking for Mark, who was unusually late. Gavin, they didn't expect to arrive on time – he was always delayed by something or other. On the far side of the park was a groundsman's hut, a broken-down relic that still hadn't been pulled down. It was left over from when there had been a bowling green and toilets. Now the park had just a playing area and the patches of grass: not much free recreation for the area. The sports complex was too expensive if you were on the dole, and besides, they'd introduced this new membership scheme to keep the scruffier kids out. Even the scrubland on the east side, which had been tarmacked to make a skate park, had been left by the Council to crack and split, because it'd been done on the cheap, until some authority had fenced it off as unsafe.

'How's your mother?' asked Trev suddenly, lighting a cigarette from a packet of ten.

'OK,' said Ricky. Why was Trev so interested in every woman, even his mother? Trev's secret life wasn't much of a secret, really. Everyone knew where he lived and how he got by. 'Were the fry-ups Mark's idea, then?'

'Yeah. Just before you joined us.'

'Why?' asked Ricky innocently. He knew Mark had recruited him because he was so thin; it came in useful, getting into difficult houses. And Mark had known from the start that Ricky wouldn't grass on them to the police, even before he'd got involved.

'Because,' said Mark, stepping unexpectedly out of the bushes behind them, 'it's a perfect meal, a fry-up.' He eyed them as if he suspected they might disagree. 'That's why. Carbohydrate in the bread and chips. Two sorts of protein – bacon and eggs. Minerals in the tomatoes. Antioxidants in the beans.' He knew his fry-ups.

Trev puffed deeply and smiled secretly: anyone would think they broke into houses for scientific reasons, the way Mark described the food.

'We could go to a caff and have one, then,' said Ricky.

'A caff?' Mark laughed.

'Yeah, they say it tastes better there –' said Ricky.

Mark's eyes darkened. 'Rubbish. Food tastes best at home.'

Trev shrugged indifferently, but Mark repeated his claim more aggressively. 'Best at home.'

'But they're not our homes,' pursued Ricky. He felt thin and vulnerable beside Mark's heftier, menacing bulk.

'They are while we're there.' No argument.

Trev nodded. 'Like holiday homes for the rich.' He knew when to support Mark and when to challenge him. He wasn't stupid.

Do we do it because we're bored? Ricky asked himself, not really thinking deeply, just letting a passing thought drift through his mind like a scrap of litter on the evening breeze. Where was Gavin? He felt happier with nervy

Gavin around; it took the pressure off him. Trev and Mark were such solid mates.

'We'll give him ten minutes,' announced Mark, as if they had something important to do or somewhere to go, which they hadn't. They never did houses two nights in a row, and without that to look forward to, the night was a blank. 'Ten minutes.'

Gavin didn't turn up, and Mark was well displeased. He wandered away towards the clock tower and the others followed, Trevor inspecting his fag packet and noting how few he had left. They were on Day Ten of their dole cheques, with no money left, but Ricky knew Trev would have a full packet by tomorrow.

By the groundsman's hut, skulking in the bushes, was the solitary figure of Ernie Steen, a greasy, lonely, shifty git who no one liked. Ernie had had no friends at school and hadn't seemed bothered. He'd always dressed in clothes from who-knew-where and hung about in the park or the multi-storey, without talking to anybody. Even his parents avoided him. The teachers had looked worried or puzzled by him, but at a distance, as if he was the sort of person you didn't want to get involved with because he'd only confuse you.

'I saw him,' said Mark, before Ricky could say anything. 'He's right strange, him. Bloody mad, I reckon. Someone should kick him one. Someone will, sooner or later.' He shot Ernie a dirty look. 'Don't trust him. He wanted to join in with me, in the early days – not that he ever really knew what I was planning. Who'd have someone like him around? Oh yeah, someone'll get him one day.'

'Someone's gonna do a lot of things one day,' muttered Trev. 'Oi, there's Gav. Gav!'

Gavin was sitting on a wall, holding his chin. It still

18

hurt on and off from the blow that morning, and he hadn't been home since he'd run out. He'd forgotten about the meeting in the park, what with thoughts of violent revenge on his dad and everything. He'd beaten up his dad a hundred times in his imagination since nine o'clock that morning, and every time, his dad had seemed to get up and grow bigger than before.

'What's up, Gav? Where were you?' said Ricky.

Gav shrugged. 'My old man hit me this morning.' And he went silent. He didn't know how to describe it.

'You're still in one piece?' asked Ricky disbelievingly. 'He's bloody huge.'

'Maybe he hit you with a cough,' said Mark contemptuously. 'He was breathing out at you.'

'He didn't!' shouted Gavin. 'He hit me full belt, and he meant it.' Silence again.

Ricky wanted to ask why, but Mark took control, brushing Gavin aside, resenting the competition.

'Now we're all here, I can tell you. I've spotted a great new house to do. Ideal.'

TWO

When Mark found a new house, they all knew what it meant: casing. As he pointed out, it wasn't just a case of getting in and out without being caught; they had to be sure the householders had the right sort of grub in the cupboards. No point breaking in and only finding spaghetti and vegetables on offer. It was surprising what sort of people were secret fans of the fry-up. Swanky business types and health fanatics might eat some fancy food with their colleagues, and then, when they got home, reach straight for the frying-pan and the oil. You couldn't predict; you had to find out.

They usually cased in pairs. Always Trev with Mark, checking out how to break in, and Gav with Ricky, doing the detective work on the person's eating habits. This new address was in Kendall Street, near the railway station.

'He's a commuter,' Mark told them, as they left the park. 'Mr Suit-and-Tie.' Mark liked to target people who were successful at work.

'Is it a risky one?' asked Gav. He was still cheesed off that Mark had overshadowed his fight with his dad.

'Don't know. We'll find out, won't we?' said Mark. 'Usual pairs. From now on, I don't want the four of us to be seen together within five streets of his house. You know why: someone always rings up the cops and says, "I saw a gang of yobbos hanging around...."' He handed Gav a quid. 'Don't spend it all in one trip.'

Gav pocketed the pound. 'What number we talking about?'

'Twelve. Fat bloke, drinks too much, great red face.

Looks dead miserable.' They reached the edge of the small shopping precinct. 'We'll split up here and meet in two hours.'

Ricky and Gav watched the other two wander off. *It's always those two together,* thought Ricky. *I wonder what other things they do. I reckon Mark must do some thieving from other places....* 'How's your chin, Gav?'

'Glad someone's fussed. That sod couldn't care less. It bloody hurt, it did.'

'You know what Mark's like, about family sticking together and everything,' said Ricky.

'He can talk. His family's a mess – his mum don't care and his dad's a maniac. He probably takes my dad's side, Mark does.'

'Probably. He's funny like that, you noticed? He blames the kids and not the parents when anything goes wrong. Dead odd.'

'Well unfair.'

'Especially when he goes on about violence. Says he hates it.' Ricky thought for a moment. It was true: Mark had never hit anyone at school. But then, nobody had bothered him. He had a kind of shield around him, a look in his eyes; he'd never needed to fight. And everyone knew how hard his dad was. You had the feeling Mark had been hit so hard so often, he wouldn't care less if somebody walloped him. Mark wasn't frightened. That thought scared people.

'Well unfair,' repeated Gavin.

'Why did your old man hit you?' asked Ricky. He was always interested in the motives of fathers, since he'd never known his own.

Gav picked up the unspoken feelings. 'You're better off without one, Ricky, mate.'

'Did you give him some lip?' persisted Ricky.

'No.' Gav shook his head. 'I've said worse. He was moody from when he got up ... funny. When he hit me, he looked scared.'

'Scared he'd knock your head off.'

'No way. I don't understand it. I dunno....' Gav paused. 'He's not like that normally, Ricky, you know. He's not one of them dads.' He didn't want to slag off his dad in public. 'I think he wants me to be a bit of a lad – you know, get drunk and all; he wouldn't mind that. Odd, innit?'

'I wouldn't know,' said Ricky sadly.

'Don't worry about it,' said Gav. 'Come on, we've got work to do. Remember: we don't get caught because we research properly.'

Ricky laughed. 'You sound like Mark. It would have to be Kendall Street, wouldn't it?'

Kendall Street was in the quiet part of town. Very residential. The residents came home from work, locked their doors, drew their curtains and stayed in. The back gardens were small and close – difficult to hide in. There was some access along the railway embankment, but not much cover. Ricky hated this area, with its silent streets and dead house-fronts. He knew he was jealous. With only him and his mum at home, their flat seemed empty and still. It didn't feel like there were enough of them to bring the flat to life.

Gavin peeled off at Neston Road and headed north, to the far end of Kendall Street. Ricky waited by a phone box at the end of a through alley. They'd take it in turns to walk along past the man's house, from opposite ends of the road, leaving a five-minute gap. A pair of guys hanging around would have attracted too much attention

22

in this area.

From his position by the phone box, he could see Gav emerging at the far end of the street and sauntering along as if he were passing through. Ricky knew that Gav would take note of any curious neighbors or nosey gits, staring out of their windows. Gav was good at noticing details without looking suspicious himself. For someone so nervous, he could look very calm and casual.

Even as Gav came closer, Ricky saw the shiny, well-painted front door of number 12 open. A red-faced man in a cricket jumper and baggy jeans came out, fiddling with a bulging set of keys.

'Mark was right,' mumbled Ricky. 'He looks a right misery-guts.'

The man locked the door as if he hated it; like a prison warder.

'Go on, Gav, follow him,' muttered Ricky to himself. But Gav had crossed the road and showed no signs of falling in behind Misery-Guts, who walked slowly and breathlessly, as if he were carrying a ton of troubles on his back; he was overweight and out of condition. Half-drunk already, guessed Ricky.

He waited while the bloke turned up towards the all-night store near the station. Looked promising. The man was your average lonely businessman, with a house and a job and a drink problem and no real friends; the sort of bloke who shopped nearby, every couple of days, because he couldn't get his act together to do a big shop at a supermarket.

Sad git, thought Ricky, feeling spiteful. Why should the man have money and a nice house, if he couldn't be bothered to make a home of it?

Ricky left his safe position in the phone box and started

trailing after him; but as the man approached the Price Freeze All-Nite, Gav appeared from a small feeder street. *Good old Gav – spotted the direction, sussed the destination,* thought Ricky. Good job, too. Gav had the quid from Mark.

When the man went in the shop, Gav followed, while Ricky disappeared down another alley to meet up back at the phone box. It was up to Gav to see what sort of stuff the bloke bought, to see if he was a fry-up man. Gav would buy some chocolate or something while he sussed out the target's eating habits. If the man, despite all appearances, turned out to be a health freak or a veggie, the disappointment would be bitter. It had happened before, though Mark usually spotted a good target first time round. Then they'd have to go through the same build-up all over again. They had to: it was their lifestyle, like a job. They worked as hard as anyone, and they worked well as a team.

'Green light,' whispered Gav from behind Ricky's shoulder, making him jump.

'Bloody idiot,' said Ricky. 'You scared the stuffing out of me.'

They sidled into the phone box, where Gav took a coin from his change and pretended to phone. 'You can see how he got that gut,' he sniped, excited. 'Does he like his grub or what? Frozen chips, bacon – best back, no less – eggs, beans, the works ... threw in some mushrooms, too. A bottle of whisky on top – full quart; right boozer. It'll please Mark. We're on a Go, now. Got a video, too.'

'How d'you know?'

'I spotted a video rental card in his wallet when he paid. Did I say wallet? It's more like a saddlebag, stuffed with notes. He's obviously loaded.'

'Doesn't concern us,' said Ricky. 'Don't let Mark hear you say that.'

'Just a fact, that's all.'

'Mark doesn't like thieving.'

'So he says. I'm not so sure.'

Ricky looked at the bruising on Gav's cheek and the lump under his jaw. Maybe not having a dad around wasn't such a bad thing after all, if they made you that bad-tempered.

👀 👀 👀

'Don't take a risk until you have to' was a rule Mark had impressed on the others. He liked to know as much about a potential house as possible, but he didn't like to get too close until the main night. He never entered the back garden of a place unless they were actually going to break in there and then. 12 Kendall Street was no exception. When he and Trevor scurried like squirrels along the railway embankment, at dusk, they kept high up, close to the line, taking a longer route than they'd take on the actual night.

Below them, the houses' backs ran in a solid jutting line, partly covered by bushes and trees. Night was coming; the lights were already on and the day's traffic fumes were clearing from the air. It didn't look like a promising area: the gardens were narrow, and every window overlooked a neighbour's backyard.

'Anyone could spot you, with this kind of houses,' muttered Trevor.

'Have to get in quick, then,' said Mark.

He was determined to do this house. Trevor guessed. 'You don't like this bloke, do you?'

'Don't know him. Nothing personal.' Mark took out a small telescope he'd bought at a car boot sale. It was his favourite possession. He loved the way it folded, neat and comfy, into its faded leather case.

They wriggled closer down the embankment towards the main wall, a thick flint-and-cement affair patched with moss and claws of ivy. An informal path ran alongside, left over from when there'd been access to the embankment for people to walk their dogs.

'Which one is it?' asked Trevor in a whisper.

'The one with the dustbin and the shed door hanging off.'

'How d'you know?'

'I counted the chimneys from the end of the road, of course,' whispered Mark. He focused on the back door and the cluttered patio: still clear enough, despite the thickening dusk. The house wasn't well looked after. He gritted his teeth: why didn't people keep their places nice? He couldn't stand that – bloody slobs.

'How's it look?' asked Trev.

'Shhh.... No alarms. There wouldn't be. Guessed as much.'

Mark swept the telescope from house to house.

'Neighbours on the north side have got the curtains closed ... other side, looks like bedrooms at the back. Kids' rooms. Could be dodgy: they might be up in the middle of the evening. Wait up – what's this?'

Before Trevor could speak, a crunching, splintering sound of undergrowth being crushed alerted them to someone approaching fast.

'Down,' hissed Mark. They buried themselves in the prickly foliage.

A figure was running quickly along the path, hidden

from view but travelling at speed – desperate speed. The figure brushed the branches and roots aside like a film monster, loud and panting, like a beast in a rage. The sound amplified as the figure burst into view. Trevor felt Mark tense and wondered how far he'd go to protect this new house, this fresh target. They mustn't be seen here. They'd have to call off the whole break-in.

The figure ran on. It was a runner in shorts and a sleeveless top, struggling along the uneven path, covered in mud and looking lost. He galloped awkwardly past their hiding-place, too concerned with his own physical pain and short breath to notice anything else.

'Close,' breathed Trevor.

Mark shrugged. 'Doesn't matter. He was lost. He won't come along here again. He looked panicked to me, like a demon was up his backside.' Again he roamed his telescope across the backs of the houses.

'No alarms,' he repeated. 'Oh, look here – the back window's open.'

'So? Plenty of people keep the windows open.' Trev reached for a fag.

'Leave the fag. Don't you see, this man's a boozer. Can't you hear his telly going?' hissed Mark. 'Full blast.'

'Maybe he's deaf,' said Trev indifferently. Mark had it in for this bloke. Trev never got involved; wasn't worth it.

Mark turned round to explain, a superior look on his face. 'Drinkers always have their stereos and tellys up full blast. The booze gets to their ears after a while, you know. And the open window – well, it's nippy tonight; no one else has got a window open.'

Trev didn't like the bitter look in Mark's eyes. No point in being nasty, he always thought; put it all behind

27

you. Trev didn't hold grudges; he forgot bad things. They slipped by him like clouds, to rain on someone else.

'A lonely man who drinks leaves the window open to clear the house,' said Mark. 'Blows away the fumes and the smell and the guilt and the failure. Works in our favour. I bet he leaves it open when he goes out. On purpose, or he forgets.' He folded away his telescope like an admiral.

Trev smirked secretly at Mark and his precious telescope, then drew a breath. 'He's coming out.'

The resident of 12 Kendall Street had shuffled out his back door in a wrinkled shirt and jeans, to drop an empty bottle in the dustbin. He looked hunched and guilty, and even from where they were spying, they could tell he'd drunk too much.

'Nice house and a good job,' murmured Mark, 'and look at him. Sad sod. I can smell his death-breath from here.'

He watched Death-Breath's movements. Number 12 wasn't security-conscious; he didn't lock the glass-panelled back door, though his silhouetted figure bent down as if to pull across a bolt at the bottom. Mark smiled contentedly. Easy.

'The problem won't be getting in. It'll be getting past the neighbours – some soft-hearted woman who feels sorry for him and keeps an eye out.'

'He needs it,' said Trevor. 'Without the suit, he's a bit of a wreck.'

Mark turned away abruptly. 'I've got no respect for him, but that's not the point. Down there's a new home for us for a night.'

'Home away from home,' grinned Trev. 'It's on, then?'

'Yeah.' Mark paused. 'But it's got to be a let-in.'

They retraced their steps back along the embankment. It would be the last time they would come that way – not that the police would bother to look for footprints, even if Death-Breath reported a break-in. They fetched up in the overgrown sidings of the deserted, dark railway yards. Twelve tracks across, in the still-operating maintenance sheds, sparks flew from the welders' guns where the night shift were making repairs to rolling stock.

Trev could see figures in safety masks and overalls stooping under the carriages, calling above the sound of the machinery and clanging tools, like a gang of aliens at work on a spaceship.

'This is the 9.24 to Venus,' he said, holding his nose to get a Martian tone.

'What?' snapped Mark.

'Nothing, mate. Joke of mine.' Trev lit his long-awaited fag and thought suddenly about Zoë. Room 317. Got her money on Thursdays: today.

They rushed over the tracks; it wasn't wise to get caught in the yards. Mark said it wasn't good news to have your name taken by the police for anything. Best to keep clear. The only computer record you needed was at the DSS, for your Social Security money. 'Those idiots who give cops cheek just get remembered,' Mark always said; 'nowadays, nobody remembers anyone who's polite.'

They skipped the broken-down chain-link fencing and hopped over a wall into Donne Crescent, a quiet street of elderly homeowners. Mark slipped off quickly towards the minor roads – this was not a good place for anyone under eighty-five to be seen loitering; old people called the cops at the sound of cats meowing. Trev was more relaxed, but he respected Mark's caution. Trev liked his freedom; he didn't want to be caught. Mark guaranteed him kicks with no comeback from the authorities – a good combination. They headed back for the rendezvous spot.

☙ ☙ ☙

Ricky was surprised. 'A let-in? Why?'

'Because it makes it more interesting,' said Mark. He looked along the cobbled shopping precinct, empty except for them and a few skateboarders. It was all closing down, anyway; nowadays there were more charity shops than real shops. No goods, no jobs. Trev, watching Mark, thought that he was almost good-looking when he was focused on something; that square, still head and those intense eyes almost made up for the difficult, superior smile.

The two pairs had joined up and swapped findings, and they were at the nervous stage of realising that another night out was a definite. Kendall Street was too good to be true. But a let-in? Why had Mark decided on that? A let-in was when just one person forced entry round the back; the others knocked on the front door, as if they were visiting friends, and were let in by their accomplice, who stayed behind the door so nobody would realise it wasn't the normal homeowner. It was risky, and Mark usually hated risks.

'I don't get it, Mark.' It wasn't like Ricky to question Mark's authority. 'It's a small street, they all know each other. Why should he suddenly have a visit from a strange bunch of lads? Someone's bound to think it's strange. Someone's bound to spot us.'

Mark was unflustered. 'The back gardens are tiny;

we'd get seen if all of us were crammed into that titchy yard.'

'Let's drop this one, then,' suggested Gav, getting jittery again.

'No, we won't,' said Mark coolly.

'There's reasons,' added Trev, picking up Mark's thinking. 'This man's wasting his house. Didn't we say this was just the sort of person who deserved it? This is more than kicks, this business.'

Gavin and Ricky nodded, though Gavin had forgotten what the more complicated reasons were. He'd really started the break-ins out of desperation, to have somewhere to go and mates to be with. He'd also hoped it might make him less scared of everything, if he lived a little dangerously. Now he wasn't sure he wasn't actually addicted to his fear, to the adrenaline rush and the terror of getting caught. In fact, he felt lost without it. He nearly said so, but he buttoned his lip.

'Who'll go in the back?' asked Ricky. 'What's the security like?'

'Security's easy, but I haven't decided who goes in yet.'

Trev sat down on a bench and took out his last cigarette. The shops around them were dark and quiet. Many had shutters down; thieving was everyone's fear. The air smelt of the hanging baskets on the lampposts, supposed to make the town centre a better, gentler place. Only the pubs at the north end of the mall seemed alive, with their heavy doors and hot windows and the punters' shouts escaping like screams from people trapped up a mountain. A wind jangled the padlocks on the shop-fronts, and a slow car backed into the Atillo's Restaurant car park. Trev lit up.

31

'He doesn't seem like the sort of bloke who ever goes out.' It was a Trev remark, Trev getting to the heart of things: why watch a loser for weeks and make all these plans, if he was going to dig in every night and stink out his own house with his own failure?

'You sound like Gav,' said Mark calmly.

'Do I?' said Trev, puffing; thinking of Zoë.

'If we'd looked at all the faults, we'd never have done anything.'

Gav didn't like Trev playing with Mark like this. If Mark decided to pack it in, they'd all have to pack it in. What would Ricky do then – Ricky with those stick-thin arms and legs of his, useful only for twisting through tiny windows or reaching awkward handles and locks? And what would he, Gav, do without the gang, without the action, without his mate Ricky?

'We're doing it,' said Mark. 'Ricky will be going in the back way.'

Gav looked at Ricky in admiration. To get Mark's trust like that was something.

'I'll take you up there soon,' Mark said. A new pairing, leaving Trevor out.

Trev puffed. The cigarette glowed. It was down to the filter. He dropped it and squashed it, glancing up at the church clock in the darkness. Ten o'clock.

'I've got to go,' he announced softly. 'Someone to see.'

Bacon. Eggs. Sausages. Frozen chips. Tinned tomatoes. Mushrooms. Black pudding. Baked beans. The man with the Sainsbury's trolley noted the traditional ingredients of a fried breakfast as he pushed the squeaking cart up the aisles. He also noted the position of the security guard, and he'd identified the store detective, who was in plain clothes – a shabby grey coat – by the cheese counter, pretending to be just another customer. The man with the trolley had sharp dark eyes that picked up every detail, and his mouth was tight and determined. His clean, neatly cut fingernails showed that he was a man who took care over everything.

The store detective, Terry Bennett, found the man suspicious. Unaware he'd been rumbled, he began to follow the shopper, suspecting a potential lifter. The man with the trolley merely smiled and continued his tour round the cold cabinets. He took out a large pack of bacon, turning it in his hands with a flourish as if he wanted everyone to see what he was buying. It looked to Terry Bennett, watching from an awkward angle, as if the man had tucked the bacon into his jacket. *Right*, thought Terry; *got him. Wait till he goes through the checkout, and bingo.*

He followed the man round the rest of the aisles; there were no more peculiar manoeuvres. *Odd thing to steal, a pack of bacon; must be a kleptomaniac.* Even odder when the man paid from a full wallet. *Not poor, then.*

'Excuse me a moment, sir. Can I ask you to stand over here?' invited Bennett, touching the man's shoulder and looking over at the security guard.

'Imbecile,' sighed the man. 'Bad eyesight, and stupid as well.' He reached into his pocket for his ID card and held it up aggressively in front of Bennett's nose. It read: 'Detective Sergeant George Tate, CID'.

And DS Tate was determined to catch the gang who were helping themselves to food in other people's houses.

After a brief chat with the manager and a quick

exchange of words – not exactly polite ones – with Terry Bennett, George Tate trundled his trolley to his car and loaded up the boot. He hadn't expected to be spotted by the gang; he was just trying to think how they did it. He got into his car and drove off.

Some of his colleagues at the station sneered about him following up these cases. All right, they weren't exactly the crimes of the century, but they bit into him. He hated any kind of theft.

'Other people's stuff. I don't appreciate that,' he muttered at the traffic lights.

He hated the idea of them lounging around in somebody else's bought-and-paid-for home. Most of all, he loathed the fact that they hadn't been caught – that was taking the mickey. And if he didn't catch them, it would be left to chance and luck. No. He was going to have them, good and proper; for their arrogance, for the cheek of it. He detested cheek. Youngsters, too – he'd worked that much out. Lazy, idle gits. Too clever to work, were they?

There's clever and there's cunning, George Tate thought. *And I've got both.*

Three

Zoë.... Trevor headed towards the Somerset Hotel, whistling to himself. *Some hotel,* he thought. It had been a hotel once, but for fifteen years it'd had a different history. Now it was split into rooms for single mothers on Social Security benefits; it was really a giant bedsit hostel, with catering facilities downstairs and a central lounge with a battered colour telly and broken-down furniture. It smelt of oil and curtains and the fog of a hundred meals cooked on rings in the lonely rooms. But to Trevor it meant comfort; it was his home, of sorts.

Zoë.... Trev had no home of his own. He'd left his parents' place a year ago and couldn't find lodgings he could afford. Here he drifted from relationship to relationship – a few weeks with one girl, a month with another – his reputation as a charmer and a Romeo going before him. They enjoyed his company; he was relaxed and easy-going, and they didn't want commitment any more than he did. If none of his contacts were around or willing, he slept in the lounge under his coat. Sometimes a stranger or a newcomer woke him, and he never refused an invite.

The Somerset's porter and general caretaker was Charlie Pitts. Charlie was a mate – as much as a greasy man in his fifties could be a friend. But Charlie was useful. He kept Trev up to date on the new arrivals and on the news of girls who'd left and gone on to better things.

Zoë.... Was she different? She had a way about her; a strength, as if she wasn't going to let this place beat her.

And she struck back at him – didn't let him get away with his easy shrugs and casual laughs.

'Evening, Charlie,' said Trev, as he pushed through the faded outer doors into the depressing gloom of the foyer. The inside of the hotel was as shabby as its decaying façade.

'Trev,' nodded Charlie from behind his desk. 'Come to light up someone's life?' He was a grey-haired, argumentative little man with a jealous glint in his eyes. 'Who's it tonight, then?'

Trev smiled but didn't answer: Charlie was useful but not likeable, and the less he knew, the better. So he just waved, went over to the dented metal lift and pressed the button. The lift clanked down like a falling coal-bunker, its door opening with a jerky screech of worn-out machinery. *Real depressing,* thought Trevor. He pushed the button for the third floor. *Zoë....* The doors rattled shut.

'Going up!' called Charlie, leaning over his desk with a leer, and his dirty cackle echoed up the lift shaft after Trevor.

Zoë. Room 317. As Trev left the lift, he heard the murmur of portable TVs behind the rows of doors on either side of the corridor. Several of the overhead lights were busted; the hall was dingy and shadowed. Not very romantic. He padded along the worn carpet towards Zoe's room, wondering for a moment why Ricky, Gav and even Mark envied him his night-time adventures.

'Ricky?'

Ricky halted on the stairs uncertainly.

'Ricky? Is that you, love?'

Still he hesitated, holding his breath.

'*Ricky!*' His mum's tone changed from friendly to furnace-fire.

'Yes,' he almost whispered.

He heard her tuck a plate into a cupboard and slam the door. 'Come and say hello properly.'

'Hello properly,' he muttered. He wanted to go straight to his room and put on the TV, or stare out the window, or stick his headphones on and swamp his brain with music. Why couldn't she leave him be?

'I'll be down in a minute, Mum,' he said more loudly.

'Where you been?'

'Out.'

'I know that. Out where?'

'Out and about. You know.'

'I know out and about could mean anything ... and probably does. When you condescend to reappear down-stairs, could you bring that dirty plate down with you?'

'I did, this morning.'

'Not the dirty plate on the bed. The other one, lurking under the cupboard.'

If she'd taken so much trouble to search it out, why couldn't she have just brought it down herself?

'Leave me be,' he whispered.

'What?'

Great, he thought. *If I shouted, 'My leg's fallen off,' she wouldn't hear; but whisper something and she always does.*

'Later,' he called. He loved his mother. He did, and he felt guilty that he wanted to be alone so much and not talk to her. But that was how it was. Sometimes she seemed so needy and the house so empty, as if she had to have him nearby because otherwise the space would terrify her. Ricky couldn't bear how much pain there often was

37

in her face, and it wasn't his fault.

Was it anybody's fault? So Dad had left years ago. So Mum was proud and strong and kept herself together against the odds. Women admired Linda; they saw how she had coped. Ricky knew, too. He knew. But he hated being the only person who could really hurt her. He wanted her to be at her toughest with him.

She was in that needy mood now, and if he tried to speak to her, they'd end up having a row. They always fought when they felt close.

She hadn't let him go yet. 'Ricky? Do you want a bacon sandwich?' She was still a voice in the kitchen. Ricky imagined her standing there, hands on hips. Her voice was calm, but he would bet she had a stormy look on her face, an electric fire in her big green eyes.

'No,' he lied. 'You know I don't like fried food.' This was one of Mark's rules: you had to pretend you hated fry-ups, as a sort of camouflage, in case anyone got suspicious.

'All right,' she sighed, and Ricky raced upstairs to his room.

He slammed the door and put a rubber wedge under it, so she couldn't just barge in. His room, in his house; with his clothes, his CDs, his skates, his books, his stuff. And yet he wanted to be somewhere else – Kendall Street, maybe: to break in somewhere, to camp, to colonise and settle himself down for an evening with Gav and Mark and Trev; a meal on his lap, knife and fork and ketchup and having a laugh under someone else's pictures on the wall. The mad shivering as he climbed a back wall, scurried over the garden, gained entry and they were in. Safe.

He opened his bedroom window and let the cold night air in. There was the smell of gardens on the breeze, a scent he knew well from their break-ins. He wanted to go out now and do it alone, but he resisted. Mark was right: planning, detail was the key.

'Ricky.' His mum was outside his door.

He sighed. 'Ye-es.'

'Mark's on the phone. Your friend. I mean, at this time of night? You'd jump off a cliff for that boy.'

Ricky opened his door. She was standing there, looking betrayed.

'Don't look at me, I'm just the messenger,' she huffed.

Downstairs, Ricky picked up the phone. Mark's voice, loud and clear and decisive, but he sounded like he needed to be quick.

'A reminder, Ricky. You'll be going in the back, at Kendall Street. Remember that.' He sounded a bit like a foreman, handing out job assignments; but really he was the boss, checking up that his men were still behind him and ready to do whatever was necessary. Tonight, each of them would get a call from Mark, so he could weigh up each one's nerve, each one's courage, each one's loyalty. 'All right?'

'Yeah. Fantastic. Why me, though? How you told it, sounded like anyone could do it.'

'But you're the quickest. Gotta go....' The phone blipped off.

Ricky's mum lingered on the landing, watching him replace the receiver. 'Not much of a call,' she said. 'Man of few words, is he?'

His mum's calls took hours and hours, words going up and down and in and out and round and round; didn't make her any happier. According to Trev, she was a good-looking woman who ought to have a lot of men in her life. And Trev should know, Trev of all people. Trev said

39

that Ricky forgot she was Mum to him, but Linda to other men.

Ricky went back to his room and stared out over the gardens, at the locked doors and shut windows – the houses and flats and bungalows. How many thieves were out tonight? How many burglars? Weren't they the people who knew how other people really lived?

He didn't feel guilty about what he and his mates did. He never had. It didn't feel like a crime to settle down in somebody else's place. More of a compliment, really, like saying: 'Your house is a nice place. Thanks for sharing it. Enjoyed it. Goodbye.' When no one invites you round, you have to invite yourself – that's what Mark said. Mark had got the idea a year back, when he visited a mate who was babysitting and realised how someone else's home was always more homely than your own – more relaxing and friendly.

We're practically house-sitters, Ricky thought, smiling. *While we're in there, there's no chance of the place being burgled, is there?*

Out in the gardens, he spotted a movement, the merest flicker of a shadow – too large to be a cat. It was a figure running doubled-up, scampering through Mrs Wellington's yard and into the Pikers'. Ricky's senses had been sharpened by practice during the break-ins; his eyes, his hearing, were always alert. It was one of the consequences of his night-time activities that he liked the most. What was the figure up to? Not thieving, that was for sure: he was taking too many risks. You didn't run along gardens to get to a back door.

The figure stopped in the darkest area of the Dellis family's yard, but Ricky still saw him; and saw him pick up a small stone and flick it at a top window. That was it, then: just another one of Sonia Dellis's boyfriends. If her old man caught him.... Sonia's dad was very protective....

Who would protect me? wondered Ricky, and shut his curtains.

👀 👀 👀

How to get Death-Breath at 12 Kendall Street out of his house? The problem haunted Mark. He didn't want to wait for the ideal night; he wanted to make it happen. Although Mark would never admit it openly, Trev had been right: Death-Breath was a stay-at-home who didn't even go out for a drink. He had a flashy old classic customised car that he never drove, not even to show off – another waste of money. There was no point in sending a fake message to entice him out: he might discover the deception and come home early, and anyway, it was one extra thing that might be traced to the four lads.

So, on Friday morning, Mark put Ricky and Gav on duty watching Kendall Street, just to see if there was any more information to be had. Trev hadn't turned up at their meeting-place, but they knew where he'd be.

Mark was faintly disgusted. 'He's got no control,' he said. 'I expect he'll roll up tonight, as usual.'

While Gav and Ricky went on watch duty, Mark went into town to see a few other friends of his who might be able to help. His first stop was Bridger Records, where Den worked on the Chart counter. Den knew all the local listings, was a member at all the clubs and, most importantly, got first call on any freebies from the record companies of band venues in town. Mark didn't like him: Den was too flashy, too trendy – a fashion follower; but he was useful, and he did Mark favours because it made

41

him feel important.

'Hello, Den,' said Mark, going into the shop during a slack period. 'How's things?'

Den shrugged. 'All right.' He was checking the latest chart entries ready for display. Despite his trendy clothes, he still looked to Mark like the same plump idiot he'd known at school.

In front of Den were piles of flyers and leaflets for various hopeful bands playing gigs in the forthcoming weeks. Mark studied them.

'Any tickets going, Den?' he asked straight out. 'I need a couple for a friend.'

Den smiled and took a box from under the counter. There was a small stack of envelopes in it.

'Everyone's running promotions this week,' he said. 'I couldn't go to all of them if I wanted to. And there's some right junk here – old-timers making comebacks, you name it.'

'Old bands, eh? 70s and 80s stuff? Can I have a sort through?'

Den pushed the box over, and Mark rummaged through the envelopes.

'What are these like, then? The Glass Beads.'

'Early 80s New Romantics – they never really made it. Bit behind the times, is he, your mate?'

'Yep – a relic. This lot? Ashkansa?'

'Heavy metal.'

'No good.' Mark couldn't see Death-Breath being tempted by that.

Mark sorted through the whole stack, realising it was a hopeless search. Den watched him, feeling like he'd let Mark down. How did Mark manage to make you feel like that?

'Cheers anyway, Den,' said Mark, pushing back the box. 'Anything else going on in town you know of?'

Den shook his head. 'I only keep up with the music scene and the record fairs. Old Tony – Tone from school, remember him? – he works in the Exhibition Centre. You could ask him. He works in the restaurant there.'

'Does he,' hummed Mark, and Den saw the dark, keen look in his eyes, the look that wrong-footed people.

Mark continued through town towards the Exhibition Centre. He couldn't afford to pay to go in, so he had to find a way round the back. Everywhere he walked, he saw people at work – serving, loading, lifting, driving, dragging, selling; sitting behind desks, standing behind counters, in suits or overalls or casual wear. A few looked happy to him, but most were just watching the clock for lunchtime. Work was for fools. He didn't need work. He didn't want it. His own free routine suited him.

He picked up an empty cardboard box from the rubbish outside a steak restaurant, fastened down the flaps and carried it round the back of the Centre to the trade doors in the underground car park. There was no real security there, except an elderly caretaker talking to an equally elderly car-park attendant, and they didn't even bother to break off their chat to challenge him as he strode by, pretending the box was full.

He pushed in through the trade doors and went along a damp, unpainted corridor into an area where unused trolleys lay in a pile by the waste disposal. Dropping his box, he split it and folded it up: there might be someone more alert than the caretaker, someone who'd find it suspicious. Then he took the service stairs up to the first floor. Once he was in the exhibition, nobody would challenge him; he'd be just another visitor browsing round

43

the exhibits or coming to have lunch at one of the town's most popular restaurants.

The carpet was thick underfoot. Mark slipped off his coat and folded it over his arm. From what he remembered of Tone, he was a thin, jerky lad with greasy hair, frowning eyebrows and weary eyes. It was hard to imagine him zipping about a posh restaurant. They must keep him hidden from sight. *Wouldn't want to put people off their food*, Mark laughed to himself. Then he reminded himself to be respectful. After all, he was out for a favour from Tone.

He passed along the plush corridors, past the conference rooms and the trade centre and the business suites, and up a wide modern staircase to the restaurant floor. It was a huge, complicated building, dedicated to promoting the town. Or so they said. Really, it was there to make the rich even richer.

Mark warily took note of the restaurant layout. Waiter service. A head waiter over by the tills; looked the sort of bloke to throw you out for mispronouncing the French words on the menu. Where was Tone? In the kitchen? Doing the dishes or chopping the salads, probably – some dead-end job. Mark picked out a leaflet from the 'Forthcoming Events' display stand and read it while he thought about how to find Tone. What was Tone's second name? Milner – yes, that was it: Milner. And Tone had a younger brother, Paul.

Mark waited until one of the younger waiters passed by the open glass doors of the restaurant.

'Excuse me ... hey – excuse me,' he said softly.

'Yes, sir.' *Sir*. Mark hid a smile.

'I – er – is Tony Milner out back?' asked Mark. 'I'm his brother Paul. I've got a message for him.'

'Tone? Yeah, he's in the kitchen.' The waiter glanced nervously at the tills, where his superior was inspecting napkins in a pedantic way. 'I can't get him.... Look, three doors along there, the white swing doors – that's the washing-up area. He's in there. Don't let the chef catch you, he'll cut your whatsits off. Be quick. Don't get Tone into trouble – he's always got someone on his back as it is.'

'Yeah, I know my brother,' lied Mark, and moved easily out of the head waiter's view.

When Mark opened the swing doors, the hiss and heat from the kitchens hit him like a blast from a sulphur spring. How could Tone work in this? The air was clammy and damp from condensation and steam, and echoed with metallic clangs and hidden voices barking orders. One foul growl in the distance was abusing some poor assistant. *Chef*, guessed Mark. *So this is the glorious thing called Work*.

To his left, in a large shadowy alcove, a bending figure hunched over a row of deep sinks, almost lost in the rising steam and choking fog. From the bony back and slicked-down hair, he recognised Tony Milner, now a full-time slave on four quid an hour. Momentarily, Mark remembered Tone at school – how he had big dreams like lots of the other boys, how he was going to conquer the world and do this and that.... *But I've got to admit*, thought Mark spitefully, *old Tone's pretty hot when it comes to washing up; look at those hands go*.

'Hi, Tone,' said Mark brightly.

Tone dropped a plate and swivelled round in the steam. Behind the metal frames loaded with crockery, pans and utensils, the raucous voices continued their unceasing shouting.

'What?' said Tone, dropping his wiry arms and wiping his wet hands. 'I remember you, from school. Mark, innit? What you doin' here? This is private. You'll get slung out.' Tone was wary, not about his job but about Mark.

'Den sent me,' said Mark lightly. 'From the record shop. Said you worked down here.' Mark had read the 'Forthcoming Events' leaflet, and now he knew exactly what he wanted. And he wanted it badly – but he couldn't let Tone see that. Tone was one for money; Mark sussed that out quickly. Tone probably worked all hours for a bit of extra cash. 'Den said you might be able to help me.'

'Oh, yeah?' Tone slowly began working again.

'He said you had contacts here.'

'I have,' agreed Tone defensively. 'Everyone knows me. I make friends easy.'

'So Den said. He told me to ask Tone, because Tone could help.'

'I don't hardly know you,' said Tone, picking up the speed of the washing-up.

'Den thought that, being a friend from school, you might help. It's not for me,' explained Mark. 'It's me uncle. He's a car fanatic – hasn't got one, hasn't got no money, but he loves all the model-building and stuff.'

He held up the brochure from the Events stand. 'There's an exhibition on Wednesday – one day only, it says; late-night special, open till ten-thirty. Models of classic cars, custom cars, memorabilia and stuff. For the collector. My uncle'd love to go, but he couldn't afford it.'

'Yeah?' said Tone. 'Why? I don't like that old stuff. What's the point of new inventions if you keep the old stuff?'

'My uncle loves it. He's out of touch.'

Tone nodded in agreement, though he'd never met Mark's uncle.

Mark decided it was time to be more direct. 'D'you get free tickets sometimes, Tone? Being a valuable employee and all that?'

Tone was wary, but he liked being seen as valuable. 'Yep.'

'Any for the Classic Cars Exhibition?'

Mark watched Tone's hands slow up in the suds. 'Yeah.... That's what you're after, then? Bloody free tickets.'

'Not free,' said Mark, noting a greedy glint in Tone's eyes.

'How much?' asked Tone sharply.

'But not money,' said Mark. 'A favour for a favour.'

'What favour?'

'The one I'll do you in return.' Mark's stare bored into Tone – not threatening, exactly, but firing a warning. Tone didn't want the tickets and couldn't sell them: they'd have 'complimentary' stamped all over them. 'One day you'll need a favour.'

'I look after myself, me,' boasted Tone uneasily. Why had Den sent this maniac Mark down here? Tone felt scared of this strange figure. What he didn't know was that Mark had meant what he said: he always returned favours.

'As it happens, I might have a spare ticket,' Tone said. He dried his hands and went to the peg where his shabby leather jacket was hanging. 'I can afford to give you one, Mark, actually. Because – because they gave me an extra ticket. 'Cause of my work record.'

He handed Mark a complimentary ticket. 'If you come back,' he said, 'you won't find me here next time. I'll probably have been promoted by then.'

'I'll move mountains to return the favour, Tone,' said Mark, heading for the door. *Another loser,* he thought. *Like Ernie Steen lurking down the park. A nothing. A nothing, made into something by contact with me.*

Outside the Exhibition Centre, he slipped the ticket into an envelope and wrote '12 Kendall Street' on it. He sauntered through town and surprised Gav and Ricky, who were still keeping a watch on the house, when he suddenly appeared on the road and quickly posted the envelope into Death-Breath's letterbox.

What's he doing? wondered Ricky, from his telephone-box lookout post.

Mark moved past Ricky, towards the alleyway beyond. As Ricky followed him into the alleyway, still wondering what on earth was going on, Gav turned onto Kendall Street to begin his pass by the house. Both Ricky and Mark spotted the broad figure of their mate, and both of them jumped simultaneously when a voice shouted from a nearby rooftop, 'Gavin!'

Gav nearly turned a somersault in shock.

'Gavin! Up here – here!'

Gav stared around with guilty, jerky movements. Finally, he shielded his eyes and looked up at the roofline. A large male figure, silhouetted against the weak sun, was waving heavy arms.

'What you doing here?' called Gav's dad from the roof.

'Nooo,' breathed Mark. 'Just what we need. It was going perfect.'

'What was the letter for?' interrupted Ricky urgently.

'Shh. Just listen. Who's that on the roof?'

Ricky hesitated. 'Sounded like Gav's dad. He must be

working along here.'

'And he's spotted Gav. Brilliant. Bloody brilliant.'

Ricky thought, *So what? Gav'll deal with it.* Why did Mark want everything so foolproof? You had to have some danger. Surely Gav was allowed to stroll down Kendall Street.

'He's only walking down the road, Mark.'

'Yes, but it's a link. Any link is bad.'

But Ricky felt that Gav dealt with the surprise quite naturally. He just stopped, had a few light words with his dad on the roof, asked if he could deliver any messages to his mum and told him to be careful. Then he asked his dad the way to Collingmore Road, pretending he was a little lost and didn't quite know where he was, and his dad gave him directions.

'Why Collingmore Road?' Mark asked.

'It's where Trev hangs out, in the hotel. Must've been the first thing that came to Gav's mind. What's the worry?'

'They said something else I missed,' said Mark. 'We'll have to head Gav off and get the complete story.' He stopped Ricky in the alleyway. 'Think I'm too cautious? You want to get caught, Ricky?' He held Ricky with his stare. 'Do you? Course you don't. Then don't question me again.' He started walking. 'It wouldn't have happened if Trev was here instead of being so ... you know how he is.'

You wouldn't have paired Trev with me anyhow, thought Ricky sourly.

Ten minutes later, they met up with a depressed Gav outside the Somerset Hotel in Collingmore Road. He was pacing up and down, embarrassed and worried that his dad might have ruined their next break-in. At least Geoff had been friendly – though it wasn't like him to work on the smaller building jobs; he usually oversaw the big commercial contracts. Maybe his business had fallen on hard times....

Mark went straight in with a question. 'What did your old man ask at the end?' he demanded.

'Why's it important?' said Gav sullenly.

'It is, because I saw your face, Gav. You looked like you'd been slapped with a mackerel. What was it?'

Gav mumbled, 'He's working late at night.'

'What!' exploded Mark.

'He asked me to warn Mum. He wants to get that loft conversion done quick, so he's putting in some late nights while the people are on holiday.'

'Bloody marvellous!' shouted Mark. 'That's it, then, isn't it?'

Then he paused. 'No. We'll change plans. Obviously you can't go in the front, Gav – you'll have to do the break-in. Instead of Ricky.'

Gav started to protest, but it was no use. He felt tremors of terror shake his body. Skinny Ricky was the expert, not him. He'd mess it up; he'd let them down; he was too nervy.

'It'll cure those nerves of yours,' said Mark with harsh finality. 'And it's definitely on. For Wednesday. I can practically guarantee that Death-Breath will be out on Wednesday night. I've made him an offer he can't refuse.' Mark laughed – an unpleasant laugh that worried Ricky, who felt everything was getting too nasty and too complicated.

'Hey!' shouted a voice from above. 'Clear off, you yobbos!'

Startled, they looked up. Trev was hanging out of a third-floor window, naked to the waist, his hair sticking up. 'I'll be down in five minutes!' he yelled.

He emerged from the front entrance ten minutes later, unwrapping a fresh packet of cigarettes and whistling to himself. He took a deep, happy breath and lit up.

'Morning, men,' he said. 'How's it hanging? Any developments?'

'Plenty,' said Ricky quickly. He wanted Trev's calming influence to kick in.

But when Mark explained the change to Trev, he just shrugged and said, 'Gav can do that, can't you, Gav? No sweat. And you're sure Death-Breath will go to this exhibition thing, Mark?'

'Oh, yeah,' said Mark. 'It's his thing. He owns a classic car, keeps it spotless. He's obviously a fanatic.'

'So he has got something in his life,' remarked Trev softly. 'After all.'

👀 👀 👀

DS Tate studied a map of the town, scattered with crosses where the fry-up break-ins had occurred. (He had a private code name for his investigation: Operation Greasy Spoon.) The only pattern he could find among the eighteen crosses was that they were all in quiet, middle-class, residential areas. Some of the houses were owned by couples, some by single people. Always houses, though; never flats.

Given his theory that the burglars were teenagers, and males at that – would girls cook greasy food? – it was safe to assume that the young lads liked making themselves at home in other people's places because they didn't like their own. So they were probably living with their parents and didn't like it much. Unemployed, too: they had to have time to case the houses, since the break-ins were slick and clever. Not a lot to go on – half the town's youth were unemployed and unhappy. No excuse. Half the town's youth weren't making free with other folks' property.

Still, Tate had a young grass with shifty eyes and an ear to the ground. Time to pay a visit to the spotty little rat. No wonder the other lads kept away from him.

👀 👀 👀

Mark watched Death-Breath polishing his car through spiteful eyes, one of them bruised from a clout from his dad. *And Gav thinks he's got problems,* thought Mark bitterly. *Well, Death-Breath, you've taken the day off, have you? To do the car up. Might that be because tonight you're going to an exhibition somewhere? I think it might, mate. And while you're gone, your home will be used for the purpose for which it was intended. My friends and I graciously accept your invite to look after it for a bit in your sad, drunken absence.*

Death-Breath looked quite chirpy, this bright Wednesday morning. After he'd cleaned the car, he hoovered the house and went shopping at the off-licence and the chemist's. He had on clean, fresh clothes and his shoes were polished.

I've brought a little joy into his life, thought Mark, smirking. He headed off to make further plans for the coming night's break-in.

Four

This was it. Gav crouched in the embankment bushes, peering across the flint wall at the row of houses; some darkened, some lit with odd oblongs of light. His heart oscillated in thin, rapid spurts; he couldn't keep still, couldn't relax. Ricky had given him the signal fifteen minutes earlier. He had ten minutes left to get in and answer the front door. If he didn't, the others would knock and retreat.

'Ricky could do this easily,' he muttered, his confidence slithering away.

But, because of his dad working down the road, it had to be him. Had Mark set up some kind of test? If he had, it was unfair. Mark never tested Trev. Trev was a law unto himself, it seemed.

Three doors from Death-Breath, a woman was ferreting about in her back garden, searching in a pile of junk, unable to see clearly in the darkness. Gav hoped a train would come by: under cover of the blasting sound, he could slide over the wall and across the garden in seconds, keeping to the edge, and dash round the back of the shed. Once he was close to Death-Breath's house, he'd be hard to spot from a neighbouring window. Getting close up was the key. And had Mark been right about the window being open?

The temperature had dropped, and a flicker of wind fluttered about the bushes. Gav's legs felt both stiff and wobbly. His hands ached. His neck was so tight, it felt like a dog had it in its jaws. From along the road came the loud, violent banging of a hammer. Dad at work.

Work, work and more work.... He loves it.

Gav checked his watch. Eight minutes left. He crawled in a panic to the flint wall and lay in the nettles at its foot. Then, slowly, he levered himself into a squatting position and peered over. *Now or never.*

He heard a train approaching. Brilliant – luck and timing! As it thundered over the embankment, Gav leapt up, rolled over the wall and dropped into the dark, untidy garden. Crouched double, he pattered along the garden's edge to avoid stumbling on garden junk: any injury could mean capture.

He tripped on a tree root and nearly cried out. It sliced at his shin like a foul tackle from a psychopathic defender. He scrunched up his face with the pain but held back his yell. *Don't give yourself away....*

'That's the last time I do the cleaning-up!' bellowed the woman three doors along, and her voice crashed about the gardens in a stampede of sound. If she didn't shut up, she'd get the attention of the police helicopter. Watch check: six minutes left.

He reached the back door and felt the glass. It was thick, difficult to break – too risky, too noisy. He had to halt for a moment and gulp in extra breath. He felt as if he'd run a marathon. He could hardly breathe, and his sweating hands left wet prints on the glass.

Was the window open?

A glimpse. He caught a glimpse of a corner of curtain flapping out of a gap under the sash window of the downstairs back room. The ledge was just above head-height, a quirk of the design of these old Victorian houses. Watch: five minutes left. He'd have to hoist himself up, lie on the ledge and push up the sash. For a minute or so he'd be completely exposed.

The woman went inside and slammed her back door. Faint shouting started up inside. A row with whoever should have done the cleaning-up.

'Come on,' Gav whispered, tensing his muscles and reaching for the sill. His dark clothes offered some camouflage, but not much. He prepared, he coiled ... he bottled out. His imagination ran mad, offering him a preview of the scratching, scraping sounds he'd make, a picture of him accidentally kicking the window glass in. Watch: just over three minutes. He had to do it. Quick. Now.

He leapt and grabbed the sill. An edge of rough stone cut his palm. Ignoring it, he pulled with his arms, threw up his leg and lurched horizontally onto the sill. Feverishly, he fumbled his arm in through the window, keeping as flat as he could. He found the inside rim of the sill, gripped it, pushed his shoulder under the window and jerked it up, with what seemed like the crash and clamour of an orchestra's percussion section. Then he rolled. And, gloriously, wonderfully, he was in, tumbling onto the carpet, catching his leg on the corner of a radiator but missing a chair and a tiny table.

Watch: less than two minutes.

Find the door. Find the hallway. Get to the front and wait. Gavin moved through the darkness of the unfamiliar room, its furniture hunched like beasts about to spring, its weird smells of polish and cleaning fluid. He groped for the door and opened it. Watch: one and a half minutes left. He was too busy, his mind working too fast, to worry or feel frightened. He flitted quickly into the hallway and down to the front door. More good luck: there was only a Yale lock, no Chubb. But then, Mark would have checked that.

At last he was there. Inside; safe; in position. The minute passed. There was a scuffling of feet outside, a cough. Then one quick rap on the door – Mark's signal. Mark never knocked long or hard enough to arouse a neighbour's interest.

Gav counted to fifteen and opened the door, standing behind it so he wouldn't be seen. In they came, their coat hoods up, obscuring their faces: Mark, Trev, and lastly Ricky.

When the front door was securely shut and the latch put down so Death-Breath couldn't get in if he came back unexpectedly, Gav half-collapsed, gasping.

'You did it, Gav,' said Ricky with genuine pride. 'Your first let-in.'

'Well done, mate,' whispered Trev, sniffing the air. 'It smells of cleaning in here. Phew. What's Death-Breath been up to? I thought he was a slob.'

'He is,' said Mark. 'Let's get to the kitchen. Ricky, the curtains – front and back.'

So they went through the same routine they'd followed eighteen times before, as a happy team. In half an hour they were comfortably camped in the living-room with their food, with the TV on and their feet up and the heating high.

'Death-Breath has done us proud,' laughed Mark, sipping a tumbler of whisky. 'Skoal.'

'You say that for beer, not spirits,' corrected Trev.

'Skoal, skoal,' laughed Mark, raising his glass. 'It's a double.' He was obviously enjoying the hospitality even more than usual.

Trev had found a box of special cigars – Death-Breath clearly liked a treat with his whisky of a night. He looked over at Mark: would a smoke count as theft?

Mark nodded – he'd let a cigar pass on this occasion. Trev laid one of the expensive, handsomely rolled cigars on his tray for after his meal.

Mark was full of praise. 'You were brilliant, Gav. Good thing I worked it out about the window.... Your old man's making a right racket along the street. Good diversion, that; he helped us out a bit there.'

'Not really,' said Gav. He didn't want his father's help in any way.

'I'm not taking anything away from you, Gav, mate,' added Mark.

Trev lifted up a sausage on his fork. 'Brilliant bangers. Very expensive brand.'

'It's odd,' said Ricky. 'How clean it is, and the good-quality grub.'

'Has he got a telly guide?' asked Mark, turning around. 'What's on later?'

'How long d'you think we've got before he comes back?' asked Trev.

Mark considered. 'The exhibition ends at ten-thirty, but I reckon he'll go somewhere for a drink, or stay and chat with the other inadequates. A boozer like that won't pass up the opportunity to sling a few drinks down. Why d'you think he didn't take his car? Never does. Remember? That's why we watch places before going in, and why we don't get caught.'

Then they jumped, startled, as someone hammered on the front door.

'Don't move,' whispered Mark, instantly in command, laying aside his plate. The banging came again.

'I know you're in there!' called a furious voice through the letterbox. 'You can pretend as much as you like. You've done it again, haven't you? Parked in a Resident's Permit space, and you haven't got a permit. Well, it's the last time! Why should I pay good money for a permit and then have to park my car in the next street? Are you listening? Next time I'm calling the clampers!'

The letterbox flap slammed down with a clatter. Mark said, 'Death-Breath doesn't seem to be very popular with his neighbours.'

Gav stopped eating. 'I'm not particularly enjoying this,' he said.

'Rubbish,' said Mark. 'Drink the whisky, it'll settle your nerves. This is the best grub we've had so far. Your stomach's bound to be a bit iffy; after all, you did the daring bit.' He raised his glass to Gav.

Gav sighed and drank the dark, aromatic liquid. It was sharp and tangy in his throat, with a fierce adult warmth and sting. Good – it tasted good; and the effect was almost instant. He felt a sudden glow and began to enjoy his pride at doing such a superb job.

He grinned at Ricky, who still looked edgy himself. Ricky was the most sensitive of them, but he'd eaten fast and hungrily – those hollow legs of his.

'Phew, I need the loo,' said Ricky, getting up and patting his stomach.

Full of food, Ricky started up the dark staircase. The smell of cleaning fluid, from when Death-Breath had strangely decided to spring-clean his house that morning, was stronger here.

The banister creaked at Ricky's touch, and he felt uneasy as he moved further away from the warmth of the front room and the hum of the telly. But it was a rule – no lights on; so he padded upstairs in the quiet gloom, peering ahead to the landing. The faint thump of hammering from four doors along hummed through the walls – Gav's dad must be driving the neighbours crazy.

Maybe if Death-Breath had a pet, it would give his home more character, thought Ricky. The house was chilly and barren, with the eerie, tragic feel of somewhere not really lived in. If he hadn't been bursting for the loo, Ricky would have dashed straight back downstairs again.

He crept along the landing, his body on red alert. The rooms exuded a peculiar deathly atmosphere. The toilet was at the far end; he leapt in and quickly locked the door, feeling safer for a moment. Death-Breath, it seemed, had even scrubbed the bath and basin. The place smelt like a hospital: disinfectant, bleach and ammonia.

Ricky forgot another rule and flushed the toilet. A shower of sound thundered about him, loud as a storm at sea, and the cistern rattled and juddered as if it was going to catapult off the wall. 'Damn,' hissed Ricky. Mark would do his nut.

Before he started downstairs Ricky glanced into one of the bedrooms, the merest look. The curtains were open, and the streetlight opposite shone a pale eye in through the window. Usual sort of furniture: cabinet, wardrobe, shelves, bed ... body on the bed.

'*Aaah!*' Ricky's scream echoed down the street. He clamped his hands to his mouth, guts heaving, legs giving way.

Before him, the room wavered in a dizzying spin, then rocked still again. But two eyes, two wide eyes, fixed him with a panther's stare from the body on the bed. Death-Breath.

Trev arrived fast and grabbed Ricky angrily; but then he, too, saw the motionless figure on the bed. He swore under his breath.

Mark rushed past them and drew the curtains. They

stood in terrified silence, listening. No running feet; nobody knocking on the door. The hammering down the street continued, violent and insistent, hard enough to bash the house to the ground.

Finally, Mark moved. He switched on the bedside light and put it on the floor under the window, so it wouldn't cast their shadows onto the curtains for outsiders to see. He hadn't lost his composure, or his anger.

'You said you saw him go out,' he hissed at Ricky.

'I – I thought I did,' said Ricky. 'Is he ...'

'He's drunk,' muttered Gav hopefully, pointing to an empty whisky bottle on the bedspread.

'With his eyes open?' scoffed Trev. 'Dead drunk. Literally. Look – there's an empty bottle of pills on the cabinet.'

'Suicide?' whispered Gav. His heart throbbed like a jet engine, and he couldn't control the trembling that threatened to loosen all the joints of his body.

They stood in silence again. Ricky, Gav and Trev looked at Mark.

He hissed, 'We didn't do it.'

'Suicide,' repeated Gav.

'Stop saying that!' snapped Ricky.

Trev was looking analytically at the man on the bed. 'He was sick – there. He might've –'

'What do we do?' Gav was shaking, unable to avoid the blank stare of the dead man, hearing his own heart pounding to the beat of his dad's hammer down the street.

'Get out,' said Mark. 'Quick.'

'Such an odd colour,' muttered Gav to himself. 'All alone and –'

'Get out, now,' commanded Mark, grabbing Gav's shirt. 'Go.'

Trev agreed. 'We'd better go. Come on. It's not our business if he wanted to die. Best get out of it. What about the plates?'

Ricky couldn't believe his ears: the plates? A dead man with his eyes bulging like two light-bulbs, and Trev was talking about crockery?

'I was sure,' said Mark tightly. 'That he'd go to that classic car show at the Exhibition Centre.'

'Front or back?' asked Trev.

Mark snapped, 'What?'

'Are we going out the front or the back?'

'Back,' said Mark. To Ricky, it didn't look as if Mark was sorry for Death-Breath at all.

The four of them had been immobilised, unable to act, but once they started to move, they felt as if a giant hand was propelling them out of the room at high speed. It shovelled them down the stairs; it sent them scrambling along the hall and threw them out the back door; it kicked them across the garden and scooped them over the wall, Ricky gasping, Gav wrenching wildly at his coat as it caught on a flint. Breathlessly they landed side by side in the sharp, cold grass of the railway embankment, each of them carrying a load of fear like a shoulder-bag.

👁 👁 👁

They should have scattered. They didn't. They huddled close and walked fast, unable to stop chattering, nervously, feverishly. For once Trev couldn't light his fag – he had to give up and put it away – and though he boasted, 'I'll have a perfect alibi; any of my girls'll vouch for me,' they could see he was shaken.

'His eyes....' said Gav. 'We didn't do it, did we? We didn't push him.'

Mark snapped, 'Shut up. He planned it ages ago. Look, he cleaned his house and his car. People do that. Didn't you know? People commit suicide because they're happy, not depressed; because they don't want to go down low again, they want to go out on a high.'

Ricky was quietest, but he murmured: 'They'll know it was us.'

'How?' Mark smiled. 'We're no one. We're nobodies. We don't exist, except on the unemployment figures.'

'My mum knows me,' persisted Ricky. 'She picks up things.'

'Well, she hasn't picked up anything so far, so why now?' Mark demanded.

Trev agreed. 'He's right, Ricky. You don't have to tell her what she doesn't know.'

He added slyly, 'Don't upset her just because you're upset right now.'

'We ate his food,' said Gav, shuddering. 'That he'd touched, you know.'

'He was alive when he touched it, idiot,' said Mark. He was afraid of their sudden weakness. 'Death-Breath's life was his business, not ours.'

'I don't think we should call him Death-Breath any more,' said Ricky. 'It's not right.'

The big question still clung to them, unspoken. It was only when they reached the safety of the park, with its camouflage of sinister darkness and thick foliage, that Trev dared ask, 'What do we do now, then?'

Mark examined their eyes; they were looking to him. He took charge.

'First of all, take your coats off and carry them. If

anyone saw us going in, they'll have seen us in our coats. Best to look different. We won't hang around together long; I'll be off in a moment. We'll meet up tomorrow....' He paused. 'You don't need to think beyond that.'

'What'll we say if anyone asks questions?' Gav wanted to know.

'Who?' demanded Mark. 'Who knows anything? Nobody's going to ask you a thing. So don't shuffle about looking guilty. Don't draw attention to yourself.'

Ricky sat down on a bench, took off his hooded coat and rolled it up; not just because of what Mark had said, but because he was hot and sweating – a mixture of fear, whisky and exertion. He said, 'Shouldn't we feel sorry for him? Death-Breath – I mean....' He caught his breath. 'He's dead, after all. And – and we were eating his food. His food.'

'Well, it's happened now,' said Mark. He was used to pain and to forgetting pain. He didn't understand why some people let it get to them.

Gav and Trev took off their coats and folded them over their arms like waiters' cloths. Mark seethed with annoyance. Death-Breath had ruined his triumph and ruined his evening. It was almost as if he had done it on purpose. Maybe that was why nobody had liked old Death-Breath.

'A waste of food, too,' said Gav half-heartedly. He was still in shock. He wanted to be back in his own room at home. 'I have to go. I want to get back.'

'Don't say anything,' warned Mark. 'Gav, keep your calm. Don't crack. Just go home and act normal. When it's light tomorrow you'll feel all right. You didn't do anything wrong. Sleep on it.'

'Okay, Mark. See you, lads.' Gav reluctantly moved

63

off towards the sturdy park gates, shivering in the chill without his coat.

'Right,' said Mark. 'You two all right? Fine, then I'm off. I'm hungry. Might be something in the fridge at home.'

And he stomped off moodily, without looking back.

It was gone midnight by the time Geoff Lindenfield got home from giving his statement at the police station, but he was quiet and reflective, rather than irritated. Watching from upstairs, Gavin sensed that his father was more sad than angry. It was such a bad coincidence that he had got mixed up in events. Gav knew his father had enough pressures to worry about. Although he knew there was nothing to place him in the street at that time, Gav needed to find out what his dad knew about the others.

Gav's mum had stayed up after her husband's earlier phone call; she knew what had happened. She'd even explained it to an innocent-seeming Gav when he'd arrived home at ten. Mags sat down on the couch with her husband; Gav could hear them clearly from the top landing. He felt a little foolish, lurking on the staircase like a five-year-old.

'Gavin's in?' asked Geoff. (*Does Dad suspect anything?*)

'Hours ago.' (*Good old Mum – an alibi.* Even though Mags was just being innocently honest.)

'What a day.'

'Why did the police keep you so long?'

'I saw something they thought might be important.' (*What? Saw what?*)

'You didn't see the murderer, Geoff!' (*Don't be so dramatic, Mum*.... Not that she ever was. She was calm, was Mum – liked to think things out. It was Dad who was the emotional one.)

'It wasn't murder. It's funny all round – complicated. It wasn't murder, though: the man committed suicide himself – whisky and pills, it looks like. Late afternoon, they reckon. What I saw was something different. See, the house was broken into at about eight o'clock. Someone got in round the back and let in three others through the front door, bold as you like. It was the three at the front I saw. Never thought anything of it, just thought they was visitors. Just a bunch of teenage lads.'

'Teenage lads? Gavin might know them.' Mags always took it for granted that her son must be popular and well known.

Geoff paused for a moment. 'It's a small town.' (*What's he getting at?*)

'Did you see their faces?' asked Mags.

'No – too dark, and anyhow they had hoods up. Could've been any of the hundreds of lads that hang around the town nowadays. Shambling around, you know....' (*What do you know about it?*)

'You seem upset, Geoff.'

'Of course I'm upset,' snapped Geoff.

'Is it the – the suicide?'

'No, it isn't! What do I care if some stranger decides to end it all? That's his affair. It's those lads. You know what they did when they broke in? They made themselves a bloody meal – believe that? A full-works fried breakfast. The police found the food abandoned in the living-room. They must have stumbled on the bloke's body and run for it. But it wasn't that that upset me. Not just that.'

'You surely don't think it was Gavin?' said Mags, shocked. (*Thanks, Mum.*)

'No, I don't – course I don't. But it could've been; it could've been. See, he's one of them, love – hanging around, not interested in work, out of touch with the real world. Any kicks'll do for them. They're in limbo or something.... I mean, you looked at our Gavin's eyes recently? Not much life in them, is there? He's got no interests. You sort of expect it in teenagers, but not in your own son. I thought he'd be growing out of it now he's seventeen. He should be full of life. Worried me, seeing them kids tonight. Probably not bad lads. Didn't pinch anything of value – didn't pinch anything except food; like they needed a home.'

'Well, that doesn't apply to our Gav.' (*Oh, no?* Mum always soothed Dad down, but that didn't mean she didn't have eyes in her head. She knew more than she let on. A deep lake, was Mum.)

'I don't know.' Geoff sighed. 'D'you think he feels at home here?' (*Dad's a bit sensitive tonight.*)

'Of course he does.'

'He hasn't got a job or anything. He's not a fool; he could work.'

'He could be working for you, but you said no.' Mags was bringing up an old argument; but she got a new response.

'I know. Starting to think I was wrong, after tonight.' (*That's a new one.*)

'Seriously?' (*Don't encourage him, Mum. Just leave me alone.*)

'I could try him out, couldn't I? I mean, he could come along on some small jobs and do the jobbing. It might get him into the swing of things. People moan about work, but the only thing worse than having a job is not having one.' Geoff paused. 'There was something else about tonight, love. The copper in charge – a plain-clothes bloke, Sergeant Tate ... he was a bit over the top. Struck me as a fanatic. He wasn't interested in the man's death at all; he was out for the lads who did the sneaky cooking. Said they'd done it before. He wanted blood, right enough; he's going to get them good and proper. I don't want my Gav ever being in the power of someone like him. You don't have to be too respectable, but you got to be on the right side of the line. You don't want sods like Tate getting a grip on you. Never.'

(*Sergeant Tate ... Sergeant Tate ... Sergeant Tate....*)

Five

For most of Wednesday night, DS George Tate had waited at the police station for any news from the squad cars out on street patrol. He didn't expect the lads to be caught; they were too clever for that. He had no doubt that the gang who'd left traces in the suicide victim's house were the same ones who had broken into all those other houses. He guessed that, when the prints came back from Forensics, they'd match. Not that that was much use: none of these lads were on file.

What concerned him most was the dead householder. Obviously it had been suicide, and the evidence showed that the man had been dead for hours before the lads arrived on the scene. So they'd found him dead. If it had shocked them too much, they might never try another break-in. DS Tate wanted them to continue; he wanted to catch them in the act.

A few of the squad cars had stopped random groups of teenagers and questioned them on the spot, but they'd found nothing suspicious, nothing beyond the usual sullen cheek and disrespect – irritating, but not criminal. No, he had to catch them red-handed in someone else's house, forks raised, feet up on someone else's furniture. He had a plan in mind.

When Ricky woke up in the lounge of the Somerset Hotel, it was gone ten. He was stiff and cold. His head throbbed and his throat was as dry as summer dirt. Trev was nowhere to be seen. In the corner, the communal TV droned out some daytime cookery programme, and there was a girl in her late teens holding a baby and smoking, with her tired eyes fixed on the screen. Ricky shifted under his coat and shivered. She didn't seem to notice he was there. Her cigarette filled the room with a drab, smelly fog, and he coughed. Had she ever been one of Trev's girlfriends? Ricky hoped not; she looked as lost and miserable as Death-Breath....

Death-Breath. The events of the night before clutched at his stomach. *Mum.* She'd be worried sick – furious and panicky both. Parts of him still felt drunk, and he was tense and bottled up. He had to ring Mum or get home quick. She'd be at work by now; he'd ring her there. Unless ... unless she'd called the police. That was the last thing he wanted. Mark always said, 'Never have any contact with the police.'

Ricky got up, rubbing his aching eyes, and put on his crumpled coat. The girl was still ignoring him, as if she were in a trance. She gave Ricky the heebie-jeebies. At least his mum had talked to him as a child – he remembered that – but this girl's baby was looking up at her in vain, if it expected a word. The whole scene made him feel even guiltier. And the smell in the lounge was the stale, rotten stink of allotment rubbish. Perhaps Trev wasn't such a lucky one with the women after all.

At the nearest phone box, Ricky rang his mum's work, trying to keep his mind clear. His thoughts slithered over each other like a tub of eels: the break-in, Death-Breath, staying out, suicide, booze, Trev's odd lifestyle, Mum ... Dad.... Part of him was afraid that something terrible had happened and things would never be the same. Another part assumed that it would just blow over and in a few days everything would be back to normal.

He got through to his mum. She was taking no prisoners.

'Where the bloody hell have you been?' He'd never heard her so angry. 'You could've – should've – rung, you didn't ring. What am I, your slave? You don't use my house as a hotel, young man, and come and go like Lord Muck as you see fit. Where were you? Out with your spotty friends, or some tarty girl dragged up from who-knows-where?'

Lots of questions, but she wasn't going to give him time to answer any of them.

'A few pence for a phone call is all it takes. A bit of courtesy, bit of respect. Unless you like to see me worried sick. Is that what you wanted? Well, you're not a man yet, and you won't be till you act like one – whatever that means. If it means acting like your father, then you can forget it. Forget it.'

'Mum –'

'And don't "Mum" me. You should've rung and Mummed me last night. I'll speak to you when I get home. You will be there? You'll condescend to spend a few minutes in your home – what's supposed to be your home?' Linda wasn't just worried about Ricky stopping out for one night. Maybe this was it: the beginning. Soon it'd be two nights, then most nights, and then he'd be gone and she'd be alone again. She'd put so much pressure on herself over the years to give him a solid life, a sensible, happy start; and now.... She thought she'd prepared herself for this, but she felt real terror. *Come on, Linda. You're a grown woman. Face it. Deal with it.*

Ricky didn't argue. It was pointless. She was off into

70

one of her rants; she could go on for hours, and anything he said would only start her off again. Best to shut up and let her nag herself into exhaustion – although that sometimes took ages as well.

'Anything you want me to do?' he asked quietly.

'Plenty. But you won't. Just make sure you're there.... You're not in trouble, are you?'

'No,' he said finally. 'I – I just stayed with Trev last night.'

'Him!' snapped his mother. 'Well, we all know about him.'

Mercifully, his money was running out. The digital counter was flicking down fast: 5 ... 4 ... 3....

'I'll see you later; I'm all right –' And the phone clicked off, out of money.

Ricky was unsure how to spend the day. He didn't dare go to the park. What was the point? It was best if they didn't meet as a group, just in case. Surely Mark wasn't expecting them to get together – but then, you never knew with Mark. Trev would probably stay in bed all day, snug in some room at the hotel....

In the end, Ricky decided to wander down to the boat pond and drift about for a couple of hours. He had just enough money for a drink, and he wanted to work out how he was going to ask Mum about his father. Despite the fuzz in his head, he remembered his chat with Trev the night before, and he was still determined to find out what his father's life was like.

As he wandered down Wallington Road, where they were doing up some old houses that had recently been squats, he heard a familiar voice yelling from an upstairs window: 'Hey, Ricky! Up here! Ricky!'

Ricky looked up and saw Gav, waving wildly from a

glassless bay window. He wore overalls covered in bits of paper and plaster, and his face was smudged with dirt.

'Gav? What you doing there?' Ricky moved closer.

Gav was holding a hammer and grinning. He tapped the broken-down window ledge with the hammer. A chunk of rendering fell into the garden below.

'I'm working with my dad for the day,' he shouted – he seemed to have completely forgotten about the previous night. 'Hang on, I'll come down.'

There was a hollow clattering of boots on bare boards inside the gutted house; then the front door swung open and Gav stepped out.

'Hello, Ricky, mate.' He coughed. 'It's filthy in there – glad to get a bit of dust-free air at last.' He shook his head, and scraps of muck flew off him. 'You're up late. It's nearly midday.'

Ricky was wondering if Gav had gone mad. He seemed to have changed his personality overnight.

'What's going on, Gav? You're acting strange....'

'Noooo,' laughed Gav. 'I'm working with me dad for the day.' Then he whispered, 'Cash in hand. Five this afternoon, I'll have money. I'll tell you what, though – they've got me doing all the hard work. I've been on the go since seven this morning.'

Ricky was dumbstruck. 'Is this – forever, Gav?'

'Just today. He decided last night.' Gav looked away. 'When he came back from the police station.' He glanced back at Ricky. 'Don't worry, he didn't see nothing.... I thought it'd be best to go along with him; but, to be honest, it's been a nice change. Something different. I'm almost enjoying myself.' He sounded apologetic.

'Would you have met up with us otherwise?' asked Ricky.

Gav looked down at the hammer, moving it from hand to hand. 'No. I think it's best we don't for a while. I mean, last night was a bit – you know ... you know what I'm saying.'

Ricky changed the subject diplomatically. 'What you doing, then?'

'Mostly knocking bits out. They're redoing three places to make them proper houses again, but you've got to get rid of the mess first. I've been ripping out old skirting boards for the last hour.'

'Gavin!' called an authoritative voice from the dingy interior of the house. 'Where you gone?' It was Geoff Lindenfield. 'Gavin!'

'I'm out here,' called Gav.

'No!' hissed Ricky. 'He might have seen me last night.'

Gavin paled. 'I forgot, I forgot. You'd better scarper. Quick.'

Too late. Geoff was in the doorway, broad and powerful, his sharp foreman's eye taking in every detail.

'Eh up,' he said. 'Distracting my workers, are you?' Ricky couldn't tell if it was a joke or a threat. It sounded like a bit of both.

Ricky smiled artificially, but inside he was panicking: he'd just realised he was wearing the same coat he'd worn the night before when Gav let him into Death-Breath's. Had Gav's dad seen him? Did he recognise the coat, and the lean body inside it? *He must*, thought Ricky; *I must be the thinnest guy in town.*

Geoff came forward, smiling. ''S all right, Gavin. Have five minutes with your mate. Get some of the dust out of you. You've done a good morning's work.' He extended a huge hand to Ricky. 'How d'you do? Ricky, right?'

'Yeah, that's right.' Ricky felt the wide palm and thick

73

fingers close around his own fragile hand and hold it in a muscular grip. This was the hand that had walloped Gav.

'So this is who you hang around with,' continued Geoff, not making any move to leave. 'Got a job, Ricky?'

Ricky shook his head, wishing he weren't wearing the telltale coat.

'Well, Gav's putting in a few days for me. Help get him into the swing of things. It's easy to get out of the habit when you ain't worked for a while, isn't it?'

Geoff was studying his son. Gav had done fine so far; listened to instructions, too. But – and it was a big 'but' – if Gav's mates lured him back into idleness....

'I'll tell you what, Ricky: why don't you join Gav down here for a couple of days? Cash in hand. Do as you're told and get on with it. No problems. No one need know.'

He stared long and hard at Ricky. 'You'll have to put on some old togs, though.'

'Sounds great,' said Gav. He was eager to have someone he knew around.

Ricky felt trapped: he had to say yes. Mr Lindenfield had the look of somebody who didn't accept the word No, had probably ripped it out of his dictionary years ago. Gav was looking at him with pleading eyes; and, besides, it might be a useful shield when Mum got hold of him tonight.

He had to agree. What was the alternative? Mark and the park? Sooner or later, Mark was going to get around to blaming him for thinking he'd seen Death-Breath leave the house.

'Yeah. Thanks – thanks. Yeah,' he nodded, with absurd enthusiasm.

'Good,' said Geoff quietly. 'Be here at seven. No later.

If you're late, that's it: you go home. No excuses, no second chance.'

And he went straight back into the house, without another word.

'He has to be like that at work,' apologised Gav. 'I've seen it. If he wasn't, the others would walk over him. There's some scary head-cases on the building sites, you know.'

'You're an expert now?' sniped Ricky, who somehow suspected he'd find the kind of hard cases who worked on a building site a bit scary.

'You are going to turn up, though, aren't you?' asked Gav.

Ricky nodded. 'Sure.' It would give him enough money to take a train anywhere in the country to visit his father. 'I'm in trouble with my mum after last night. I didn't want to go back; I stayed with Trev at the hotel. It might smooth things over if I tell her I've got a few days' work.'

'Gavin!' called the voice of authority again.

'I'd better go,' said Gav. 'See you tomorrow. I won't be at the park later. If you go, explain to Mark. Tell him I'm too tired. I will be, an' all.'

'Okay. If I go.' Ricky had no intention of meeting up with Mark; not tonight, not for a long time.

☯ ☯ ☯

It didn't take Mark too long to realise the others weren't coming. It was nearly dark and the park was deserted. Even the usual regulars seemed to be elsewhere. Maybe there was a party going on. Mark didn't get invited to parties. He didn't have any contact with anyone but the other three. It was the sort of secret best kept to a small group; and it isolated you from everyone else.

Anyone watching Mark would have seen how annoyed he was. His lean, hard face was even tighter and more intense than normal, and there was a hurt, bitter look in his eyes.

And someone was watching him: the only other person in the park, by himself as ever. Someone had a lot on his mind and a lot of money in his pocket. DS George Tate had filled both of them. Tate had said to him, 'I want you to keep an eye out for groups of four lads. Got that? Groups of four. Any foursome that sticks together and keeps themselves to themselves. Any gang like that, you report to me. Give me some names, and don't mess me about.'

Someone knew Mark fitted into that category – him and his three mates; always hanging about, planning something. So why was Mark alone tonight? And why did Tate want information about four lads? Someone thought he might get a nice bonus if he could find out a few facts; but he wasn't about to approach Mark Wills. He sensed that Mark Wills despised him – and, besides, he could find out as much from a distance. He was good at a distance. He had to be. He was never close to people.

When he looked again, Mark Wills had gone, disappeared into the darkness. Right fast, too. You couldn't trust anyone who could lose himself that quickly.

DS George Tate was a happy man. He'd just been given the go-ahead for his plan to catch the breakfast thieves.

Maybe he'd presented the lads' behaviour as more calculated than it was, suggested it was having a bigger impact on the community's confidence in the local police force than it actually had; but his Chief Superintendent had been sufficiently impressed to say yes. Having a suicide victim in the middle of the case had helped. The press had got hold of the story, and the local paper was poking around for information about juvenile delinquents and the crime rate among the young unemployed of the town. Suddenly Tate's personal obsession was public enough to demand some fast action, and he'd been given a couple of officers to help him clear it up swiftly, before it began to look like the police couldn't catch a gang of teenagers who liked a bit of night-time cooking. The fact that Tate had leaked the information to a journalist friend was best left a secret.

Tate had a plan, and now he had the personnel and a month to wrap things up. It shouldn't be a problem: the breakfast thieves had averaged two break-ins a month for the last nine months, so he wouldn't have long to wait. He thought about the exact instant in which he'd nick them. He pictured it clearly, in great detail. They'd be smug and arrogant, lounging around the way young lads do, scoffing the stolen food and laughing about the absent householder. No doubt they were so cocky, so sure they couldn't be caught, that there wouldn't be a lookout. Then, *bang* – he'd have them. He longed to see the look in their eyes when they were surrounded, with no escape and no excuses and quite literally with egg on their faces.

He had no wife, no kids of his own, and his impatience with teenagers was well documented. He couldn't leave them be; it was as if he wanted them to grow up into adults straightaway, skip all the nonsense of their youth.

He quoted the research: 'Most crime is committed by men under twenty-five.' He wanted to change that statistic, single-handedly.

☯ ☯ ☯

'I was thinking about you yesterday,' said Zoë, sitting down at the little table by the window. She'd made egg on toast for breakfast. They always sat by the window; somehow it made the dingy room seem bigger, more airy.

'Oh yeah?' smiled Trev. He was already smoking, though he'd only been up five minutes. He looked mildly into Zoë's eyes. They were a glorious green, still lively and full of fun, despite all she'd been through.

Zoë played with her short auburn hair. She said she kept it short because two-year-old Allie threw her food at mealtimes, but Trev thought the cut suited her small face and figure. She said, 'It's great to have a lie-in, without Allie to get us up early. I've got to go and collect her from Aunt Jenny's in a couple of hours.'

'I'll go with you,' said Trev lightly. 'So you were thinking about me, then?'

Zoë laughed. 'Yeah, but probably not as much as you were thinking about you.'

Trev grinned. 'Yeah, I was,' she said. 'I was thinking that you've got this bit of your life here and you've got other mysterious bits somewhere else, and I bet none of the bits know about the others. You like to keep 'em all separate, Trev, don't you?'

Trev shrugged. 'Maybe.' But he was startled at how right Zoë was. He knew she was sharp, but she'd surprised him again.

'Eat your egg,' said Zoë. 'It's nice for me to make

some food for an adult for a change.' She touched Trev's hand. 'Here, you're not offended, are you? It wasn't a criticism.'

'No. Fine,' said Trev genuinely. The truth was, it sort of moved him that someone had bothered to think so much about him.

'You – you don't do anything ... you know, horrible ... in those other parts of your life, do you, Trev?' asked Zoë. 'I mean, you're a great lad, you know....'

'Course I don't,' said Trev, hoping the egg and toast in his mouth would hide the lie.

She leaned over and kissed him before the conversation got too heavy. They said Trev was a right Romeo and a sleep-about, but she'd never felt so respected by a boyfriend before; and that was important to her, after her past. Not that Trev made a song and dance about it. One day, she thought, Trev might be a great dad. It wasn't going to be with her and Allie, and that broke her heart; but he was with her this morning, and Zoë had learned to enjoy what was good, while it was good.

They were at it again; the builders.

'You'll never lift that with that arm.'

'I've seen more fat on a bacon rasher.'

'It'll snap off – better use both hands....'

Ricky blushed and lifted the pint of beer. Gav, sitting next to him, kept quiet, grateful it was Ricky taking the verbal battering. All morning, the other three site workers had been on at Ricky, ever since he turned up to work. It was his thinness; it made him an easy target. Gav guessed they were easier on him because his dad was the boss, but Ricky – 'Sticky', they called him – got the full works. Yet at lunchtime they'd invited Gav and Ricky down the pub with them for a beer, so maybe it was good-natured.

'I'm glad you came,' said Gav to Ricky, when the other three went to play darts. 'I didn't think you'd turn up. You didn't seem keen yesterday.'

'I had to. My mum went crazy yesterday, completely stressed out, when she got back from work. It was the only thing calmed her down, when I said I had a few day's work.... It's a bit like being back at school, innit? Getting a nickname and having the piss taken all the time.... So this is work.'

'They do it to everyone. They do it to each other. I've listened.'

'Yeah. I suppose so. Bit different from hanging out, innit? I'm aching already. I've been up and down those ladders I don't know how many times.' Ricky added in a lower voice, 'They're doing it on purpose. Like a test. Initiation ceremony.'

'Well, don't get narky. Take it for my sake. Remember the dosh at the end of it ... and they did pay for the drinks. You're too sensitive, Ricky, mate.'

'At least you didn't call me Sticky – it's so childish.' Ricky took a huge swig of his beer. Wasn't this what a lot of the lads at school had dreamt about in their last year? Keeping fit and hard from physical work, a few beers at lunchtime, money in your pocket. 'I don't know why I didn't go on to sixth-form college. I had the grades. What happened? I don't remember deciding not to go.'

'You must do. You said you never wanted to hear a bell again as long as you lived, or sit at another desk. You said it over and over again,' Gav reminded him. At the time, not having the grades or the choice himself, he'd admired Ricky's rebellion.

'Did I?' Ricky took another huge swig.

'Take it easy. We've got a long afternoon's work ahead, you know.'

'A long afternoon of insults, yeah.... Gav? Listen. When I stayed at Trev's hotel – well, not his hotel, but you know – we had a talk about my dad. I haven't seen him for years. I'd stopped thinking about him. Trev made me get guilty about it. So I've decided I'm going to try and find out where he lives and everything. That's why I'm earning this money. In case I need to travel there.' He coughed and stared at Gav. 'What d'you think?'

Gav looked towards the dartboard and hesitated. 'I can't imagine what it's like not having your dad around. Mine's never off my back. It's different with Trev – it's hard to think of Trev ever having a dad....' He paused. 'How will you find him? I mean, if your mum won't tell you, or she doesn't know.... It might take years.'

'The Salvation Army. I've heard about it. They can trace anyone.'

Gav laughed. 'The Salvation Army?'

'Yeah. They're brilliant at it. If Mum doesn't know, they'll find him.'

'Oi, Sticky!' yelled a voice from the darts corner. 'Fancy a game?'

'If he can lift the darts!'

Ricky whispered to Gav, 'Should I?' And they both smiled. Badminton, tennis, cricket, darts – Ricky had perfect hand-eye coordination.

'Go on,' said Gav. 'Show 'em no mercy. You might make some money.'

On the way back to the houses, Ricky counted his

winnings. Fifteen pound. All in all, Frank, Dave and Jeff had taken their defeats very well. Mind you, they hadn't been fooled – they'd seen he was a good player right away; but they wanted to get a game off him, and they didn't mind losing a few quid for it. With the earnings from two days on the site, he'd have enough to go anywhere in the country. And it was important to Ricky that he'd proved to the men that his wiry little arms had strength. Gav had watched the whole thing unfold, smiling to himself, eager to tell his dad over dinner that night.

Once back in the house, though, Frank took over again and had the two lads rushing here, there and everywhere. He might have an inflated view of his skill at darts, but he knew which jobs needed doing and where. Ricky was glad to get up a sweat and work the drinks out of his system. The day galloped by at high speed.

And then the next day sped by too, and Ricky got his money from Gav's dad. He bought his mum a small bunch of flowers on the way home and left them on the kitchen table, a little embarrassed ... a lot embarrassed. On the Saturday night he stayed in his room, too tired to come downstairs. He lay on his bed wondering how to ask her about his dad. That could wait until Sunday lunchtime. He had other things to think about.

It was odd working with Gav. It was like the last eighteen months hadn't existed. What was Mark doing? And Trev? Trev, the great survivor.... Ricky wondered if it was all right to earn some extra cash for a short while. Would Mark think of it as a betrayal? And could he do it for the rest of his life? Going down the pub with the likes of Frank, Dave and Jeff? You could only be Sticky Ricky for so long. Maybe Dad would have an answer.... Maybe he wouldn't.

Ricky wasn't sure what he wanted from his dad, when he found him. What would be good and what would be bad? Dad might be an idiot; Dad might be an expensive disappointment. Dad might be a vision of his own future that he'd rather not know about. As he lay alone in the darkness of his room, he realised that the time had come to start thinking again; to think his life through once more. It had been so easy to drift and dream without direction. It was like he'd sunk into something soft that had seemed like a warm, inviting mattress, but which was really cold mud, clinging onto him, sucking him down.

At eleven the phone downstairs rang, and he heard his mum answer.

'Who's that? Oh, Mark – my Ricky's friend.... Well, yes and no. He's not well. He's gone to bed early. He's asleep.... No, I can't go and wake him up. Certainly not. You'll have to ring another time.' She put down the phone and muttered, 'Cheek.'

Upstairs, Ricky smiled. Mum could still be protective, and she'd guessed, with that instinct of hers, that tonight he was best left alone. He turned over. His shoulders, back and legs ached from the hard physical work.

If I did it every day, would I put on muscle? he wondered to himself, half-asleep. It was a funny idea. In his drowsy state he imagined himself built like a truck, with sideburns like hedges, stomping down to the police station in a huge suit, lifting up benches, pulling shop doors accidentally off their hinges and denting a car with a friendly pat. He laughed quietly in the soothing darkness. The cool duvet on his burning muscles ... the echoes across the gardens ... sleep.

The next morning, Gav rang and wanted to meet up; just the two of them. He sounded upset and jittery.

'Ricky. Guess who rang last night?'

'Mark,' said Ricky.

'How d'you know?'

'He rang here too. I was half-asleep. I could hardly move.'

'Tell me about it. Me too, but he was like a maniac – shouting and screaming. I had to put my hand over the receiver in case Dad heard. He called me a traitor and a grass.... He wants to see us, but I don't want to. I don't think we should all meet up for a while. It's dodgy.' Gav paused. 'I'm sort of trying to forget it.'

'He's just worried,' said Ricky. 'We should've told him what we've been doing. It's completely innocent.'

'But, Ricky, he was real threatening. You don't think he'll blackmail us?'

Ricky tried not to laugh; he felt strong after his long, deep sleep. 'No. Get a grip, Gav. If he did that, he'd have to admit everything himself.'

'Yeah. Maybe. But he sounded so crazy – I thought he'd be happier if we were all done, rather than him be alone.... Are you free, Ricky? We can meet up somewhere. Come on – meet me at the Brock Inn. You haven't got the excuse about money.' Gav's voice was pleading. 'It's nearly twelve. Meet me there.'

He was being a bit silly, Ricky thought. After all, Mark hated the authorities; he wouldn't grass on anyone, however angry he was. All the same, he said, 'I'll see you there,' and put down the phone.

'Conflict?' said a voice behind him. It was Mum, dressed to go out and looking sharp.

Ricky nodded.

She looked at him steadily. 'You don't stay with the same friends forever, Ricky. Not many people do. People go their separate ways.'

Well, she knows all about separate ways. Look at her and Dad. 'I forgot you know everything,' Ricky snapped, forgetting Saturday's flowers and good intentions – she could be so irritating!

'Thanks for the flowers.' She smiled. 'That was a change. Got any more work with Gav's dad coming up?'

'I dunno.'

'Well, don't mess it up. Keep on his good side; it might lead to something more permanent.... And I don't think much of that shifty article who rang here last night – Mark whatever. Keep away from him, as far as you can. Though I've got time for that Trevor. He's a charmer – not to be trusted, of course, but a good heart.'

Ricky was already walking away. If he stayed, he'd ask the question – *Where's Dad?* – and he wasn't up to the fallout yet. It was Sunday, and it'd been a pig of a week.

When he got to the Brock Inn, Gav was waiting in a dusty alcove, looking so guilty that Ricky had to say, 'Gav. Relax. We're underage, remember? You look so guilty you could hang for something.'

'Got served, no problem,' said Gav, getting his pride together. 'Just 'cause you could've got into sixth-form college, doesn't mean you know everything.'

'What you getting at me for?'

'Dunno. Sorry, mate. Sit down. Maybe we should move away from the windows, eh?'

'What for?' Ricky felt Gav was even more jumpy than ever.

'In case Mark goes by.'

'You're getting right paranoid. So what if he does?

85

We're allowed to meet, aren't we? You can bet your boots Trev is lying low in the hotel.'

'S'pose so. Let's move anyway; it's a bit bright here. Hurts my eyes.'

Ricky laughed. 'All right. Fancy a game of darts?'

'You're joking,' said Gav. 'Against you? Waste of time.' He moved into a quieter corner and relaxed a little, now he was hidden away. 'What'll we do, Ricky, mate?'

'Nothing. We haven't done anything. Besides, I've got other things on my mind.'

'I forgot. Your dad and all that. Sorry.'

Gav waited while Ricky bought himself a beer, but it was obvious he couldn't wait to get things off his chest. As soon as Ricky returned, Gav said, 'I'm not scared of Mark, really. It's just that last break-in, and the body....'

He paused. 'See, if Mark asks me to do another one, I'll do it. You know I would. I reckon I'm addicted, Ricky. Addicted to it. The last few days, even though I've enjoyed the work and the dosh, I've been thinking about the high of getting into a strange house, and the fry-up and everything....'

'Then we'd better both make sure we keep away from Mark,' said Ricky. He was addicted himself, he realised suddenly; but addicted to the thought of finding his father.

Six

In disbelief, DS George Tate peered through the window of the interview room. 'And what exactly is that, Kingston?' he asked.

Detective Constable Kingston, young and confident and eager, smiled. 'It's him. We got him – caught him in the act. In the kitchen, egg sandwich in hand.'

'Is that so?' replied Tate dryly. 'Let's go in and see, shall we?'

Tate dismissed the duty officer from the room and sat down opposite the suspect, while Kingston stood in the corner behind him. The prisoner glanced around nervously and fidgeted on his chair, hands tapping the table. He was a sad sight, with his overgrown grey beard, his stinking overcoat and his grimy hands. His face was wrinkled and tanned from years of living out in the open, but his eyes were still quick and sharp. Obviously, it was hell for him to be cooped up in such a small space; he was used to the roads and the sky. *An old-fashioned vagrant*, thought Tate, *the sort you don't often see nowadays; they've been driven out by the new, younger, more violent breed of beggars.*

'I only had an egg sandwich!' yelled the man suddenly.

'I know,' said Tate, who could see bits of it still stuck in the man's beard and down his coat.

'It was already made.'

'So you thought it was a new sort of takeaway, did you?'

'I was starving hungry,' explained the man, who clearly had no intention of hiding anything. 'The door was open, and I just popped in to take it. Nothing else. In and out, it was going to be ... but I – I forgot. I sat down and drifted off. Don't know why.' The blazing smell of cheap sherry on his breath seemed like a good enough explanation to Tate.

'You'll be charged, of course,' said Tate. 'Is this the first time you've done this in this area?'

'I've done plenty of other things,' said the man. 'But I don't go near houses normally. It was just the opportunity got me. I was starving hungry, and I just forgot and –'

Tate got up. 'Kingston. Give him a reprimand. Then fetch him a sandwich from the canteen and kick him out.' He turned back to the man. 'And you, if I see you again – I don't care if it was salmon mousse and duchesse potatoes that gave you your "opportunity", I'll have you up and inside before you can uncork a bottle of meths. Understand?'

The man nodded. 'Thanks, Sergeant. I was starving hungry, and I –'

But Tate had marched off to the door, throwing Kingston a look en route that said, *We'll speak about this later, Constable.*

👁 👁 👁

Gav's dad had to go oversee a job in another town for a day or two. He seemed reluctant, and he wanted to take his son with him. His wife couldn't understand the necessity.

'Geoff, leave him alone. He'll be all right here with me.'

Geoff shrugged his shoulders. 'I s'pose so, love. But he's got a bit of a taste for the work now.'

'He'll still have a taste for it in a few days' time, I'm

'sure.' Mags wanted a bit of her son to herself while Geoff was gone.

'I would take him, but I'm going to be on the go the whole time. Can't afford to supervise him.'

'Well, you haven't even asked him if he'd want to go, Geoff. You can't just order him about as you like. He's seventeen now.'

'Don't go spoiling him,' warned Geoff. 'Don't let him blow all his earnings.... On second thoughts, let him blow the lot.' He chuckled. 'Then he'll need to earn some more.'

'I'll let him make his own mistakes,' said Mags. 'You just give him the chance to make them good again afterwards.' She was pleased at her husband's change of heart, glad that he was involving himself with Gav's future in a more practical way than simply bullying and moaning. Even if Gav needed a bit of that sort of pressure now and again, it was nice to see Geoff showing more directly that he cared. She knew he did care; she just wished Gav realised it too.

Geoff smiled. 'Make his own mistakes.... You tell me all about it, love.'

It was early Monday morning, before seven. Geoff was packed and ready to go. Gav came downstairs, dressed and wide awake. His few days of work had got him into the habit of not sleeping in; to his surprise, he'd woken up at 6.45, feeling fit and full of energy. Now it struck him that there was a long day ahead and not much to fill it with. He envied his dad, his appointments elsewhere.

As he came into the kitchen Geoff asked, 'What'll you do today, Gav?'

'Dunno. I'll probably ring Ricky and see what he's up to, maybe.'

'He seems a sad sort of lad to me,' said Geoff. 'A look in his eyes.'

'He's got things on his mind.' Gav hesitated. 'To do with – with his dad.'

Mags was listening carefully. 'His dad doesn't live with them?'

'Ricky hasn't seen him for years,' said Gav, wondering if he was betraying his friend.

'And now he wants to,' finished Geoff. 'That's natural. Everyone wants to know where their parents are. Hope he ain't disappointed. Might turn out to be someone like me, eh?' He laughed uneasily. 'Anyway, I've got to go. Want to miss the rush-hour traffic. I'll ring later.'

Almost as soon as Geoff had departed, the phone rang. It was Ricky, sounding agitated and nervous.

'Gav? That you? It's Ricky. Sorry to ring so early. Couldn't sleep.'

'Me neither. Woke up without thinking about it. You sound odd, mate.'

Ricky paused. 'I feel odd. Look, are you free today? I want a favour.'

'Course I am. As long as it's not meeting you-know-who.'

'Well ... it is, actually.'

Gav was surprised. 'I thought you didn't want to see him either.'

'What? Oh – not Mark,' said Ricky. 'My ... my dad.'

Silence. Gav didn't know what to say. 'Today? You're meeting him today?'

'Yeah. I've found out where he is. I want you to come with me, on the train – for company. You don't have to see him. You can have a beer somewhere.... Look, you've got to come. Just say yes, and I'll explain later.'

'Of course I will. Yes,' agreed Gav, trying to sound absolutely certain.

👀 👀 👀

The middle-aged woman behind the supermarket checkout watched Trev pack the shopping into three plastic bags. She nodded approvingly at Zoë.

'You've got him well trained,' she said.

'He's self-taught,' smiled Zoë, worried that Trev might take offence. Trev felt he should be annoyed, being talked about like that; but, oddly, he was more proud than angry.

They'd taken Allie out to the park for the afternoon; Trev and Zoë had watched her in the sand, on the swings, going down the slide and hiding in the funhouse. A simple, contented few hours. Quietly normal. Real. He'd held Zoë's hand a lot, casually caressing her fingers.

He kept thinking it was time to leave the pair of them and saunter off alone, as he usually did, but something stopped him each time. First Allie wanted a lolly, then Zoë needed the loo, then he was the right height for steadying Allie on the slide. Now they were shopping, he wanted to help. After all, Zoë had a hard life, all work and duty; why not give her a bit of support for once?

'He's not my dad,' Allie suddenly told the woman.

A hunched, hurt sensation creased in Trev's stomach. He'd been happy; now he felt an unfamiliar pain. He hid it from Zoë, who was checking her change. For a moment, he wished he were Allie's dad.

Outside, Zoë kissed his neck. 'Sorry,' she whispered.

'What for?' said Trev lightly.

'Well, that woman ... she thought we were – you know,

91

a married couple or something. I thought you might be a bit annoyed.'

Trev shrugged and glanced down at Allie. 'No. Me? Why?'

They walked on towards the hotel. Zoë looked secretly sideways at his lean, handsome face, his intelligent dark eyes. She knew he'd have to go soon. *That's what happens,* she thought, *when you're not truly together – you're parting all the time.* She wondered if Trev felt the same.

'Shall I stay for tea?' asked Trev suddenly. 'Yeah?'

'Great,' said Zoë, surprised. 'Allie, Trev's gonna stay a bit longer.'

Allie hugged his leg and he had to stop walking. Looking down at the little girl, he felt strangely special.

'Urgh,' said Allie.

'What's that for?' Trev asked.

'I don't know.' Zoë smiled. 'Something, I suppose.'

Staying put in one place, sticking it out with one person: that was the sort of life that had always filled Trev with terror. But something was changing in him. This afternoon, in the gentle hours at the park and now strolling along, he felt the seduction of stability, normality. Perhaps it wasn't so boring after all, wasn't so much of a trap. Perhaps it took a different sort of daring, a different kind of courage.

It was only after the train pulled out of the station that Gav could get an explanation from Ricky. He was clearly in a bit of a state, so excited and terrified that he fidgeted around in his seat like a dog with fleas.

'Calm down, mate,' said Gav. 'You're making me jumpy

too. What happened? Did your mum tell you? This is all going too fast for me. I mean, did she just decide to tell you?'

'Not exactly,' said Ricky, and told Gav the full story.

The previous night, his mum had been pacing about downstairs; even from up in his room, Ricky had realised she was fretting about something. At first he didn't want to go down and get involved. It might be one of her emotional scenes, which went on and on; she'd be better off ringing her friends, the way she usually did. But she didn't telephone anyone. That worried Ricky, and at last he reluctantly left the haven of his room to see what the matter was.

As he went downstairs, he suddenly realised he wasn't used to starting up conversations with his mum. What would he say? How to begin? She might not want him to interfere....

He was about to retreat again when she called out, 'Ricky? You coming down?' She paused. 'I wanted to have a word – not a nag; you're safe from that. Come in here.'

She was sitting on the couch, looking small and worried.

'What is it?' asked Ricky warily.

'You're a sensitive boy,' she began. He flinched; he hated that kind of comment. 'I – I was watching a TV programme today....'

Oh yeah, thought Ricky, *here we go: some rubbish about out-of-control teenagers, or something.*

'It was about – I mean, it made me think. I've been meaning to ask you some things, for a long time. But I didn't want to.'

'It's really annoying when you do this,' said Ricky rudely, 'instead of saying what it is. Just say what it is.'

93

'I am,' his mother flared up. 'In my own way. You're so impatient.'

'I'm supposed to be, I'm young,' he said sarcastically.

'All right. I'll just say it, then.' Linda hesitated again. 'Yeah, very clear.'

'You cheeky little – you don't know everything, you know –' Linda had been fiery before Ricky; maybe she'd be fiery again when he was grown up ... properly.

Ricky sat down. 'I don't want to argue, Mum.' He sighed. 'I never do, but you sort of bring it on.' He saw the hurt on her face. Was that one of the accusations Dad had thrown at her, all those years ago? 'Mum, I wanted to ask you something as well.'

There was a deep silence between them. Until she laughed.

'So who's going to go first, then? Or shall we wait all night?' She sat still and put her hands in her lap, desperate to be in control of herself.

Ricky coughed and launched straight in. 'I want to see him.'

'Him?'

'You know who. I want to find out where Dad is and see him – just see him. Just see what he's like. I don't remember him much, even though I was ten when he left.' Ricky studied his mother's face for her reaction....

The train rattled over a viaduct as Ricky finished telling Gav the story.

'Did she burst into tears?' asked Gav, whose mother sometimes did.

'Not at all.' Ricky grinned. 'It was amazing. She practically yelled with joy. I couldn't believe it.'

'I don't get it. She wasn't upset?' said Gav.

'No! She was relieved. That's what she'd been worrying

about. She couldn't understand why I hadn't asked about him before. She didn't think it was natural. I reckon she was scared that she'd been stopping me somehow – "emotional blackmail" was what she said. Come to think of it, I haven't seen her so happy in years.'

Gav thought about it for a moment. 'She's right, though: it was odd. Be honest, mate – it was. Until Trev mentioned it, you never said anything about your dad, really. I mean, I've never said anything before, but I did wonder ... you know – what you felt, and all.'

Ricky shook his head. 'Seems like everyone's been saying nothing for ages.'

Gav stared out the window, embarrassed: should he be going with Ricky? 'Does your dad know you're coming? It's all a bit sudden.'

'No, he doesn't. I'm just going to turn up. Don't know why – I just want to turn up. Mum's known for a couple of years where he was, but she's been waiting for me to ask. I think she's a bit tormented about it.'

'He might be a loony,' said Gav, in his direct way, 'and throw a major stress.'

Ricky ignored him. 'Strange, him living so close. I might have seen him before without realising it. Mind you, if I'd known, I might have been staring at every skinny middle-aged bloke who walked by and wondering if he was the same blood type as me.'

Gav was getting more nervous. 'How many stops to go?'

'Four.' Ricky took a huge breath. 'Look at my hands; they're sweating. I've got sweat all down my back. Breaking into houses is less nerve-racking than this.' He paused. 'I wonder what Mark's been up to for the last few days.'

'Don't mention it, Ricky,' said Gav. 'I'm not going to

do it again, me. When my dad gets back, there'll be more work.' He touched Ricky's shoulder. 'Thanks for paying my fare. I blew all me earnings last night. Went out alone – mad, really; drank a skinful and bought a takeaway. I'm practically skint again.'

'Dear oh dear.' Ricky smiled. 'You're falling into the trap Mark goes on about. You know – people work so hard, and they hate it so much they have to spend all their dosh to get over it, and then only work can save 'em by earning them some more dosh to blow again to get rid of the misery of working.... Round and round, he said.'

'Round and round,' echoed Gav. 'I must be a round-and-round person.' He brightened. 'Loved it, though – being off my face, forgetting everything for a while.'

The train reached Levant Halt and they got off. Gav gathered his torn coat around him; it was cold. He wanted to get rid of the tear in his jacket; it reminded him of how he'd ripped it at Death-Breath's house. Death-Breath who was gone now. Not breathing at all, any more.... Had Death-Breath gone round and round? Gav shivered. The thought frightened him too much.

But Ricky was picking up his pace, looking about with interest.

'Why's he live here? Why here? It's a nothing little town. He must have a good job somewhere roundabout.' His thin face looked as drawn as a string bag. 'Come on, Gav. Here we are.'

Outside the station, a single rusty taxi slept in the rank and the trees underhung the unpainted railway fencing. It was as if the small country town was closed like a shop, shutting down. Gav wondered what Ricky wanted his father to be. Having a friend along might give you support, but it'd be embarrassing if your dad was a total write-off. Gav didn't want to see Ricky get hurt.

'Do I have to come any further?' he asked.

'Not really. It's only – it'll be a bit boring if you have to hang around here all day. If it takes all day. I don't know where the house is from the station.' The truth was that now Ricky wanted to be completely alone, and he felt guilty for dragging Gav all the way out here. It seemed cruel to say, *I don't want you around any more, Gav; this is my business.* 'You could always poke around and see if there's anywhere worth casing.'

'Don't say it. Even as a joke,' said Gav. 'I might get tempted.'

He scanned the roads. There were likely houses everywhere. No way should Mark get word of this place; he'd be on the train and poking around in no time. 'I'll just have a cup of tea and take it from there, mate.'

Ricky took out a fiver. 'Have a drink, Gav. Take it – I've got plenty for now. Anyhow, you said your dad'll have more work.' *Take it,* he thought, *and leave me be. I've got to be by myself.*

Gav took the money and folded it into his pocket. 'When'll we meet back here? You could be any time.'

'If I'm not back by four o'clock, just go. If I'm coming back, I'll make sure I'm right here by then. Hope it's not too boring for you.'

Gav laughed. 'Unlike the incredibly full days we normally have?'

'Thanks, Gav. See you later, then.'

'Cheers, Ricky, mate. Don't get your hopes up too much.'

'I won't. I'm only coming to see. I haven't got any wild plans.'

Ricky headed briskly off towards the bus station, to

ask directions. He could hardly control his shivering, or the cascade of thoughts and questions and images that crashed through his mind. The ideas joined up into a kind of whirlpool, until a car hooted, bringing him back to his senses; he'd walked right by the bus station, into a garage forecourt.

He stood still for a moment, to calm down and to remind himself that he didn't have to see this through if he didn't want to. He could go home to Mum and lie. Now he was so close to seeing his father, it seemed like an incredibly stupid and unnatural thing to do.

But he asked at the bus station's Information desk, and the woman said, 'Couston Avenue? The Number 37 takes you right there.'

A 37 bus was waiting in the terminus, and the driver was clicking the ticket machine, ready to depart. Ricky sprinted across to it. Once he was in motion, he'd feel confident again.

Charlie Pitts came up from the basement of the Somerset Hotel, plunger in hand and nostrils still full of the reek from unblocking a drain. He was not in a good mood. What on earth did they stuff down the toilets and sinks upstairs? The plumbing was too ancient and faulty to take the waste from so many rooms. And what did he get out of his job? Nothing. Big fat zero.

As he emerged from the basement steps into the lobby, he spotted a solitary figure loitering by the reception desk.

'Hey, who are you?' challenged Charlie, waving the smelly plunger. 'Ain't seen you before.' Charlie Pitts was too stupid to be a coward, and besides, he didn't like people on his territory.

'Sorry, mate. Didn't mean to startle you. Beg your pardon.' Mark didn't make eye contact, to ensure Charlie felt secure. 'I've come to find Trevor; I'm a friend of his.'

'Oh, are you?' Charlie sounded annoyed with Trev; Charlie sounded annoyed with the whole wide world. *All the better*, thought Mark.

'I haven't seen him for a good few days,' said Mark.

'Who has? Dirty little beggar – treats this place like ... like a hotel,' grumbled Charlie, putting the filthy plunger on his desk.

'Sounds like Trev,' said Mark sympathetically. 'Nice bloke, but a bit self-centred.'

'Self-centred – I'll say.' Charlie looked at Mark. 'So he lets his friends down and all, does he? Wouldn't surprise me. Only thinks about one thing.' He moved the plunger with a squelch.

Mark nodded. 'So you haven't seen him either, then?'

'Nope. He's up there all right. Doing his rounds of the girls, no doubt.'

'Does he help you out here, then?' asked Mark innocently. 'Odd jobs and stuff?'

'Does he heck,' said Charlie, and paused. 'Now, I hadn't thought of that, you know. Hadn't thought. I must be soft. The favours I do him – and has he ever done anything in return? Like heck he has. I'm glad you mentioned that, I am. He bloody should, really.'

'Sounds reasonable,' agreed Mark. 'You ought to insist.'

'I'm going to,' announced Charlie, not realising he was already in Mark's trap. 'What's your name, then?'

'Mark.'

'Pleased to meet you.'

99

'Me too.'

'Well, there you are – I ain't seen him for days.'

Mark faked disappointment. The truth was, he'd actually come to see Charlie Pitts.

'I'd better go, then. See you, Charlie.'

'How d'you know my name?'

'Trev told me about you. Mentioned you quite a bit.'

'Did he, now?'

'Uh-huh. I hope you don't mind me saying ... but you're not a bit like he said, now I've met you in person.'

Charlie looked suspicious, wary. He was an insecure man. 'Yeah?'

'No. You seem fine to me – not at all bitter and twisted.'

'What?' snapped Charlie. He gripped the plunger. 'Is that what he –'

'No, no – don't get me wrong! Trev just thinks everyone's jealous of him.'

Charlie exploded. 'Jealous! Me jealous of that streak of –'

'It's just Trev's way. Arrogant. He don't mean it,' said Mark, watching Charlie go purple with hatred and rage. What an easy man to manipulate.

'I'll give him jealous,' shouted Charlie, ignoring Mark. 'Ungrateful little beggar! I'll give him – Right, that's it!'

He headed for the lift, shouting to himself. Mark watched the angry little man furiously stabbing the lift button with the plunger and striding into the creaky lift with revenge on his mind. He smiled and quietly walked out of the hotel.

Charlie Pitts strode along the corridor to Zoë's room, blowing steam, and hammered on the door with the plunger.

'Open up! Zoë? Zoë, it's Charlie! Have you got that

Trevor in there with you?'

There was a scuffling noise inside, some whispers. Then the door opened and there stood Trevor, calm, confident and smiling.

'Hi, Charlie,' he said.

Charlie spat out the single word. 'Out!'

'What!' said Trev. 'What's the matter?'

'Out.'

Trev sized Charlie up; the man had gone haywire. 'What for, Charlie? Why should I? The women here are allowed anyone they like in their rooms, whenever they like.' He smiled. 'You don't have any power over their lives ... much as you'd like to, I'm sure.'

'You toe-rag!' screamed Charlie. 'Get your clothes and get out!'

'Shh,' said Trevor. 'There's kids asleep all along the corridor, Charlie. Calm down, will you?' He couldn't believe Charlie was really serious.

'You get out now and don't come back, ever. Or I'll call the police. You're of no fixed abode. Whose address you been giving to the Social Security, then? That's fraud, that is. That's years behind bars. Now shift.'

Trev turned pale. Charlie had gone nuts; but Charlie was right, and Charlie had the upper hand.

It was beyond Trev's dignity to rush. He wouldn't give Charlie the satisfaction of seeing him panic. He said, 'All right, Charlie. If you like. I'll be off.' His guts twisted at the idea. 'But it'll take me a few minutes, you know.'

'Right, then, Romeo,' said Charlie. 'I'll sit downstairs, and if you're not past me and out the door in five minutes, I'll be on the phone before you can say goodbye-and-kiss-my-you-know-what.'

Five minutes later, from his hiding-place across the

101

road, Mark watched Trev's departure from the Somerset Hotel. He heard a few hasty exchanges of words and saw Trev raise his fists at a small figure waving a plunger. He saw Trev button up his coat against the night chill and light a rebellious fag on the steps and stare up at the third floor, and finally trudge away down the street.

Lovely. That's one back on board, Mark thought. *Two to go.*

● ● ●

What did Ricky remember about his dad? Not much. There wasn't much to latch onto. His father had been away working a lot, weeks at a time; and when he had been at home, all those years ago, he had always seemed to be tired. He rarely made the effort to go out with Ricky. In fact, he seemed to be permanently stuck in some adult world where kids didn't figure. Even at eight years old, Ricky had realised that his dad somehow distrusted children and preferred to be with grown men; he didn't even have much time for his wife. But he hadn't been a grumpy person, or nasty. It was just that he wasn't made for family life, and he saw it as some kind of mistake that he was supposed to be at home and talk with the people there. In the end, things had been easier when Dad wasn't there – more normal. Every time he had come back, it had just upset the routine....

These were only vague memories; Ricky had to struggle to remember even that much as he walked slowly, fearfully, up Couston Avenue.

Just a quick visit, he reminded himself. *Just to see – just to see.*

It was a posh street; big houses with bay windows and

long front gardens. Clearly his father had money. *All that work, I suppose*, thought Ricky sourly; *all that work, and you get a big front garden and trees for it.* Not for the first time, he re-ran a fantasy of his: everyone with a young family was paid by the government until the kids were ten, so both parents were always around for the early years....

Ricky counted down the numbers on the even side of the road: 186, 184, 182 ... heading towards 96. He calculated how many houses to go. He wanted to be there; he wanted to be back home with Mum. What a silent street – no noise or bustle. Did Dad like quiet when he came home from work? Or was he always away on business, like he had been in the past?

Ricky halted for a moment and blew out a few breaths. It was hard to stay calm; your body wouldn't let it happen. He was outside 96. After a second's hesitation, he grabbed the iron gate, flung it open and strode down the path. The garden was tidy and the house well decorated; the windows were clean, with security locks, and there was a burglar-alarm box perched under the gutters, over the top left-hand window. Ricky smiled: Mark's training didn't seep away after only five days.

He had no idea what he was going to say. He simply rang the bell and waited, watching the coloured panels of the frosted glass in the top of the door. A wide shadowy head appeared behind the glass, and the lock clicked. Ricky held his breath.

The door opened. A man looked out; he was holding spectacles in his left hand and he wore a business shirt and tie. Ricky stood rigidly, terrified, unable to speak. He stared at the familiar, unfamiliar man.

'Yes?' asked the man. 'Can I help you?'

Ricky cleared his throat. 'Yes ... um ....' He breathed in. 'Mr – Mr Naylor?'

The man nodded.

'I'm ... I'm –'

'Ricky,' said the man. 'Ricky.' His voice was business-like.

'Yes, Ricky ... your son.' Never had Ricky felt so absurd, as if he were telling a lie, as if he were a con artist out to blackmail this man. His mind raced: *Does he look like me, do I look like him, is it obvious we're related?*

'Come in,' invited the man. *My father.*

Ricky stepped into the hall. The man seemed to be keeping as far away from him as possible; they were acting like they were scared of each other. His father put his glasses on, then hastily took them off again. He tried a smile but thought better of it. He looked as though he expected Ricky to attack him.

He held out his hand awkwardly. 'Hello,' he said. 'Ricky....'

Ricky looked at the clean smooth hand and didn't know what to do.

'Linda – your mother rang,' admitted the man. 'She thought you might come here.' He coughed. 'So, to be honest, I've been sort of expecting you.'

Ricky couldn't bring himself to move. He couldn't speak. He just stared at the man – his father – a fit man, a man with grey eyes and big ears; a man who'd spoken to his mother.

'You knew I was coming,' said Ricky, suddenly wanting to smash the house to pieces. 'No one told me.'

He could see his dad was sizing him up, noticing the thinness and the anxiety. 'Not easy, eh?' said his father. 'I'd say, "Have a drink," but I don't keep any in the house.' He thought for a moment. 'I could ask Mrs Dawson to get something from the off-licence.'

'Who's Mrs Dawson?' asked Ricky blankly.

'She's my housekeeper. I'm away on business a lot. She keeps things ticking over.' Ricky could tell that this was something the unfamiliar man had said many times before.

Will he say anything new to me? wondered Ricky. *Will he?*

Seven

Trev was in a rage. His normal calm was shot to pieces. In one evening Charlie Pitts had taken away his security, his base and his refuge. What had got into Charlie – or, more importantly, who had got to Charlie?

Trev had a fair idea. It was Mark: Mark, up to some sly, slimy scheme. Mark hated being ignored or having his plans interrupted. Mark didn't care about any of them; all Mark cared about was the break-ins and carrying on his own private battle of revenge against the world. Well, Trev could see how revenge might be a sweet thing. He could beat Mark at his own game.

But Trev was practical, a survivor, and his raging didn't last long. When he thought about it, Charlie Pitts wouldn't be at the hotel forever. And Charlie Pitts had secrets of his own that the owners of the property might not approve of. So all wasn't lost there. In the meantime, though, Trev was even more homeless than before. The weather was mild, so it wasn't too much of a disaster; but he had to find some kind of temporary shelter, just for a few days – a week at the most.

When Trev had first left home, he'd spent weeks hiding out in the allotments near the railway. Some of the sheds there were quite fancy, with armchairs and electric points. A couple had hidden bottles of booze that the owners stored there to keep their habits secret. Trev had learned to pick padlocks or find ways into the less secure huts. He decided to try his luck there again. It irritated him, because it was a backward step; but it wouldn't be for long. His plan of revenge was already forming nicely, and he had a feeling it wouldn't be long before that snake Mark made contact.

It was dark by the time he reached the fence around the allotments. Everybody was long gone from their plots. It looked much the same as it had nine months earlier; it was the sort of place that didn't change. Trev could have been depressed by the sight of it and the situation he was in, but he drew on the inner toughness that had kept him going through every crisis in the past. *Big deal,* he thought; *I've always had to fend for myself anyway.*

Besides, he could still contact Zoë....

Trev clambered quietly over the rickety chain-link fence and padded swiftly along the unkempt paths, towards the back of the allotments, where there were covering trees and he would be a long way from the street. He knew which shed he was heading for. If the plot hadn't changed hands, he expected to find blankets inside, and some biscuits; there used to be a camping stove, too, and a kettle for making tea. *Almost all the home comforts,* he thought grimly.

The door had the same padlock – perhaps a little more battered, a bit more rusty, but Trev had no trouble picking the lock with the thin blade he carried everywhere he went.

I'm always creeping about or breaking in, he thought suddenly. For the first time he tried to imagine what it would be like to stop, to sort out something more permanent.

He pulled the door to behind him and wedged it shut. The twin windows even had roughly made curtains on them. He drew the curtains and slumped on the battered armchair in the corner, remembering the smell of compost and plastic and vegetables and the steady aroma of the shed's wooden walls. It was safe to smoke, if he was careful; and Trev was always careful.

His hatred of Mark returned. He was more and more sure that Mark had wound up Charlie Pitts, who was too stupid to get wound up by himself.

Trev lit the camping stove with his lighter and put the kettle on. A vague gassy smell filled the shed. While he waited for the kettle to boil, he dug out the blankets – yes, they were still there too – and laid them out on the chair. The biscuits were kept in a tin, he remembered, next to the sugar and milk containers; there was no milk this time, but he found a packet of gingersnaps – and, tucked away at the back of the shelf, a half-bottle of cheap brandy, still three-quarters full.

Five minutes later, he was wrapped up in the armchair with a mug of black tea heavily laced with brandy, working out the details of his plan.

I'm going to get away from this town altogether this time, he thought. *Far away, and start fresh somewhere else.*

He could get some money from Zoë. Maybe a little extra from some of his other girls, but not much. He'd have two weeks' benefit money. The rest would have to come from another source. *Another source....* Then Trevor tensed.

Outside. Outside he heard the faintest of sounds, the tiniest rustle. A footstep, sounding loud and unnatural in the deserted wilderness of the allotments. Trev put down the mug and unwrapped himself from the blankets. Somebody was moving around the back of the shed; someone trying hard not to make a sound.

Trev smiled. The person had found the front door and was trying to lift the latch.

'It's all right,' said Trev. 'Go on, Mark. Open it.'

108

There was a pause. Then the door opened slightly and Mark looked into the dark interior of the shed, where only the glowing tip of Trev's cigarette cast any light. 'How'd you know it was me?' asked Mark.

'A night watchman would've had a torch, and the owner – I've seen him: believe me, he would've crashed straight through the door and grabbed me. Come in quick, before someone stops you.'

'I'm glad I found you,' came Mark's voice in the blackness. 'Isn't there some light in here? A candle or something?'

'There's a camping light,' said Trev. 'On the shelf. I never used it. I liked the darkness – helped me think ... about stuff.'

Mark fumbled about for the lamp and found the switch. Its light was dim. 'The batteries are low.'

Trev smiled. 'I didn't know you were scared of the dark.' But he deliberately kept any hatred out of his voice.

'Well, I'm glad I found you. I just went to the hotel and saw that bloke – what's his name? Charlie? – and he went haywire, told me to clear off and said he'd chucked you out. I was worried.'

'Were you?'

'Yeah. I thought, where will old Trev go? Then I remembered here. I thought it was worth a try – and here you are.'

Trev sipped his tea, puffed his fag. 'Except,' he said at last, 'I never told anyone where this place was, did I? I only ever said I lived out on an allotment somewhere. Which means – doesn't it, Mark? – that you followed me here. And you followed me because you knew I was going to get chucked out by Charlie Pitts, because you bloody well made sure that I did get chucked out.'

Mark said nothing. He wondered if it was worth lying about, but he decided that Trev wasn't really that annoyed.

'I know why you did it,' said Trev, more gently. 'You were worried the team would break up because of Death-Breath. But you only had to talk to me, mate.' He sighed. 'I was a bit pissed off, but I'm not now. It's probably for the best. I was getting in a rut at the hotel.'

Mark nodded warily. 'Yeah – yeah. I considered that, Trev.'

'We should carry on doing what we do best, yeah? And as soon as possible.'

'You got somewhere in mind?'

Trev shrugged. 'Well, not yet; I've seen a few likely places, though. Tomorrow I'll have a quick look around. What about Gav and Ricky? We want the whole team.'

Mark was still cautious. 'They've been working for Gav's dad. I mean, proper paid work. I can't believe they've joined the slaves.'

'Not for long,' said Trev. 'I reckon they'd do one last break-in. A kind of farewell. I know I could persuade Ricky. Gav's just a bit scared because of Death-Breath, but they'll soon get fed up with work after the first excitement's worn off.'

Mark felt his leadership being tugged away from him. Trev seemed so definite, so confident. But Mark desperately wanted to keep the team going, and if Trev could manage that, well.... *Besides,* thought Mark, *let him do all the work this time; let him feel like he's boss for a bit. When it comes to the crunch, we'll see who leads and who follows.*

'You staying here tonight?' asked Trev.

'No way. It smells in here,' Mark said. 'Don't know how you stand it.'

'I bloody well have to. Anyhow, look, I'll have a look

around tomorrow – maybe find out what Gav and Ricky are up to – and I'll meet you in the park at four, all right?'

'No hard feelings?' asked Mark.

'None,' said Trevor, sipping his brandy-laced tea.

Gav's mother was interested. The men of the household were certainly behaving oddly this week. First Geoff had changed his mind about giving Gavin work; and now, all of a sudden, Gavin wanted to sit down and talk about his friend Ricky, when usually it was a struggle to get him to grind out two words together.

'He didn't come back at the time we'd arranged,' said Gav.

'So you think he'll stay with his father?' Mags asked.

'I don't know,' said Gav, puzzled. 'It was well strange him wanting to go in the first place, out of the blue, after all these years. And then taking me too....'

'It's called friendship,' said Mags.

'I s'pose so.' Gav looked miserable.

'You know what's wrong with you, Gavin, don't you? You just want to know what happened. Can't bear to be left out of it. A bit jealous, maybe – having to share your friend with his dad.'

'Rubbish,' snapped Gav. 'Ricky said he just wanted to see his old man, to see what he was like and what he did. That's all.'

'Maybe,' said Mags. 'I wonder what happened.'

'See, you're the same.'

The phone interrupted him, and he sighed as his mum went over to answer it. He was worried about Ricky.

111

Suppose Ricky's dad had turned out to be a maniac. Suppose Ricky had done something rash, or was so disappointed he'd gone off somewhere to escape from things....

Mags returned. 'That was Geoff. He's going to be gone a few days – this damn job. He's got to sort out some mess or other. He said when he gets back, you can start work again on the site – not until.'

Gav flared up. 'Breaking his promises again. He promised he'd be back tonight and I could start again tomorrow. Typical. He never meant it.'

'Calm down, Gavin. It's only a couple of days. You're keen on work all of a sudden, aren't you? One extreme to the other.'

'So what?' said Gav sullenly. The truth was he'd run out of money. And he wanted more; he could get addicted to spending – he liked it. Also, there was Mark. Gav felt he needed the work to go to, to keep him away from Mark and the temptation of the break-ins: they were addictions he needed to drop. He felt unprotected – and now even Ricky wasn't around to support him.

'Don't look so worried. Ricky'll be back. Probably on the late train.'

'I'm not worried about that.'

'What have you got to be worried about, at your age?' laughed his mum.

Gav shouted, 'Why do you always say that? I'm worried, all right? If I'm worried, I'm worried – whether you think I should be or not.'

'You're a rude little beggar sometimes, Gavin Lindenfield.' Mags stood up. 'For a moment I thought we were going to have a decent chat.' She stormed off into the kitchen.

The phone rang again, and Gav dived for it: it might be Ricky.

'Hello, Gav? Mark here.'

Mark's voice paralysed Gav. 'Yeah,' he said slowly.

'Haven't seen you for a while. Look, I'm ringing because Trevor asked me to....'

'Trev?' That caught Gav's interest.

'Yep. He's got a problem. He wants to meet you and Ricky in the park – usual place. He's a bit embarrassed, so he asked me to ring for him.'

Gav felt invisible chains closing in on him, and there was no Ricky to help him resist. With Dad away and Mum in a strop, what else was there to do? He was bored....

Mark continued lightly, 'I've got to go somewhere, but I said I'd pass on the message. He'll be there in half an hour. If you can't make it, well....'

'I don't know,' said Gav desperately. At least only Trev would be there.

'Well, I'd better go. See you sometime – whenever.'

Gav put down the phone. His mum's voice floated out from the kitchen.

'Was that him – Ricky?'

'No, it was Mark.'

'Oh, him. Don't like him. Too greasy by half.'

'He's all right,' said Gav defensively: what did she know about his friends?

'Not who I'd choose for a friend,' her voice nagged.

It irritated Gav. He whispered, 'Well, it's not up to you, is it?'

'Keep away from him, I would,' she called, unaware of the effect she was having.

Gav decided quickly. 'I'm going out!' And he was

through the front door before she got out of the kitchen to ask him where.

When he arrived at the park, Trev was sitting on a wall, looking less well-kept than usual. His hair was plastered down, and dark rings circled his eyes, as if he hadn't slept for days.

He didn't say hello; he simply acknowledged Gav with a glance and seemed to drift back into a private daydream. That drew Gav in.

'What's up, Trev? You look down. Something wrong? Mark rang.'

'Did he?' muttered Trev carefully. He glanced at Gav. 'You still upset about what happened at Death-Breath's? I am.'

Gav was surprised. 'You? I didn't think you'd....' He didn't want to accuse Trev of having no feelings. 'I've been thinking about it a lot.'

'Me, too. Pity ... we had some fun before, didn't we?' Trev sighed. 'I don't suppose we'll do it again now. Not even Mark.'

'That why you're down?'

'No! Not just that. Charlie's gone bonkers and banned me from the hotel.'

'Where you living, then?' Gav asked. 'You haven't gone back home?'

'Course not – they wouldn't recognise me. I'm in temporary accommodation.'

'Through the Social Security, sort of thing?' said Gav innocently.

'No, you prat. I'm back in the allotment shed.' Trev lit a cigarette. 'Bit of a come-down from the comfort of the bloody Somerset Hotel.' He drew on the cigarette and looked at Gav. 'I'm thinking of leaving town altogether,

114

making a new start somewhere else.' He watched Gav's reaction carefully.

'You can't do that! We're all mates – a team.'

'Not any more,' said Trev. 'That's all finished, since Death-Breath. Sad that it had to end up on such a low note. Pity about that.'

Gav stuck to the subject. 'You can't go off without any money. Maybe my dad'll give you some work,' he added hopefully.

'Come off it. He can't take on every unemployed lad who comes along.'

'So your mind's made up.' Gav felt a sudden emptiness hollow out his stomach. Was everything falling to pieces suddenly? And no Ricky....

Trev noted Gav's sadness. 'Yep. I'm going.' He paused. 'It would be nice to have a send-off, you know? I sort of mentioned it to Mark – I said we could do one last break-in, as a kind of farewell – but he didn't seem that keen. Pity.'

'Didn't he?' Gav was startled.

'No. Maybe he's lost his nerve and doesn't want to show it,' said Trev.

Gav thought about it. 'One last time....' He liked the idea. 'Just one last one, to round things off. I think I could do that. If I could do it, I'm sure Mark could.' He looked at Trev. 'And that would be it, wouldn't it?'

'Have to be,' said Trev. 'Since I'll be leaving town after, and I s'pose you and maybe Ricky'll work for your dad.'

'You're definitely going, then?'

'Definitely. I spent today putting a few plans and ideas into operation. Busy old day, I've had. Very useful. Very.'

'What sort of things?'

'Can't say; it'd be embarrassing if they didn't come off. But I've spotted the perfect place for the break-in. Cased it myself already.'

'That's quick.'

'Well, it's perfect. A young couple; I heard the neighbours saying they're out every night, down the clubs till late. Ideal.'

'Except,' pointed out Gav, 'there's no Ricky.'

'Who's that, then?' said Trev, pointing to the distant park entrance, where the unmistakeable thin figure of Ricky was coming towards them.

👀 👀 👀

Ricky had missed the earlier train. He'd spent a long and often awkward day with his father; Dan. It had been an odd meeting, and Ricky had stayed on and on, lingered, hoping the strangeness would wear off and he'd come to some kind of decision about the visit.

At first Dan had been nervous and restless. He was a slim man, fit, with large brown eyes and a habit of chewing his bottom lip. He seemed to start talking in the middle of sentences.

'... And so here we are,' he said quietly, when he'd led Ricky into the kitchen. He acted as if he expected a big row, lots of blame and anger thrown his way. '... That, actually ... your mother did ring me to wa– to tell me she thought you might be coming. Hope it doesn't spoil the surprise for you.'

'It's all right,' said Ricky, calmly sitting down. The kitchen was fitted, done out in an old-fashioned style; almost luxurious.

116

Dan sat down, then jumped up. 'D'you want to see round?'

Ricky shook his head; no, he did not. He wasn't a house-buyer.

'Oh,' said his father. 'Cup of something? I was just about to break off from some work myself.'

There was a silence. *Who is this man?* wondered Ricky, fishing around for something to say. He felt blocked up, filled with concrete. His mind was empty.

'I haven't seen you for eight years,' said his dad suddenly.

'I know.'

Dan winced. 'I didn't see you much before that.'

'I guess not.' Ricky felt that if he let go his feelings might get out of control. But what did he feel, anyway? He didn't know this man, and the man barely knew him.

'I expect,' started his dad, 'I expect you've got lots of questions.... You're very quiet.' He studied his son's thin face. 'I was – well, worried: I sort of expected you to come in shouting and screaming at me, demanding to know this and that.'

Now Ricky felt sullen. 'I could try it if you like; if it'd make you feel better. What's your job?'

'It's hard to explain. It's a business-type thing – you know: lots of paper and meetings, too much coffee and late nights.'

'Not very interesting, then,' said Ricky sourly. 'What did Mum say? I didn't realise you two spoke to each other.'

Dan shuffled on his chair. 'We don't. There's not nastiness between us, you understand; there's sort of – nothing, really. Like we were never married. But no bad feelings, I don't think.' He was aware that that sounded

117

bad to Ricky. 'You'll be eighteen pretty soon, won't you? I don't know if I should say this – your mother doesn't know – but, well, I put money in a fund for you, for when you're eighteen. Quite a lot. A good start, financially speaking.'

Ricky thought, *A present from a stranger.*

'I don't hate you,' he found himself saying. 'I haven't missed you. You can't miss someone you didn't know.' He knew he was deliberately being cruel, and he watched his father's face register the pain.

'I wasn't made for a family,' his dad said. 'I shouldn't have tried. I thought it was the best decision, to keep right out of it and let your mother bring you up. The best way, yes. It gets so complicated and muddled up any other way, it seems.'

'Oh, I see,' Ricky flared up. 'Another good business decision, eh?'

'No, no. Not like that. It was better for me to be gone.'

'Completely,' said Ricky. It was beginning; he could feel it – a great, uncurling, rearing wave of feelings. He wanted to stop. Let his father be right; let there be nothing between them. 'Glad you sorted out your mistake so neatly, then.'

'I don't know what to say,' admitted Dan blankly. 'A man can be good at other things than being a dad.'

Who's he reassuring – me or himself? Ricky struggled to feel some kind of bond with his father, but it couldn't be forced. Finally he said, 'Okay. Show me round, then.' He took a breath. 'Who decided on my name – you or Mum?'

'We both chose it.' And Dan got up.

After the first excruciating hour, the tension eased gradually. Dan had an office at home, and it helped when

118

he switched off his computer link to his company, showing that he was completely available for Ricky for the rest of the day. Ricky started to find it easier to let the questions and emotions arise at their own pace; and, as the afternoon progressed, he was able to piece together a picture of his parents' marriage and separation. About his father, he learned more of what he already knew: that here was a man obsessed with work, a man who couldn't relax; who had found the one thing he was excellent at, and committed all his waking hours to it.

Ricky realised with a sense of sadness that his dad was a man, not a myth: a one-sided, single-minded man for whom relationships were alien, difficult things and feelings were something other people knew more about, something best avoided. If Dan had stayed at home, what would have been different? There'd have been the same distance, the same empty stretch between them; except, Ricky admitted, he'd have been even more resentful and would probably have caused trouble to get back at his dad.

He wondered if any of this was crossing his father's mind, or if his dad had the ability to simply shut out any ideas that might upset his balance or interfere with his business. Dan offered to pay back Ricky's train fare (Ricky accepted); he tried some apologies, occasionally glanced nervously at the switched-off fax machine, and enquired politely about Linda's situation. Mum, it seemed, had never asked for maintenance or made any attempt to draw his father back to family life. So she'd played her part in the situation, too.

So all these years, without realising it, I've just gone along with what the pair of them wanted, Ricky thought.

Eventually Ricky knew he had to leave; and, staring into Dan's face, he knew they weren't going to make any great efforts to see each other again. That was just the way it was. To know as much as he'd found out seemed enough.

He said goodbye with a generous handful of banknotes in his pocket. Leaving the splendid but unlived-in house, he felt almost sorry for the odd figure on the doorstep: his father – not a heartless man, but a man who'd never found his heart and likely never would. *I must get everything from Mum*, thought Ricky, *unless Dad is good at darts*.

At least now he could put a face and a life to that word 'Dad'; and it was clear that Dan hadn't left because there were others he had stronger feelings for. There were no others; there were no feelings.

Riding back to the station on the bus, Ricky – stunned and empty – decided that he'd be as emotional as he could; that he'd have millions of friends, love every woman he saw, be affectionate to Mum. He also felt his old anger returning: anger towards work, that beast, that all-devouring creature that ate and ate and chewed up every bit of your life it could, like it had eaten his father's.

☯ ☯ ☯

If it hadn't been heartbreaking it would have been funny, the way Ricky stamped about trying to shake out his anger. He wasn't even specifically angry with either his mum or his dad. He was just furious with his situation and the whirl of his feelings. It didn't seem fair that he should have to feel them at all, when all of this was his parents' fault.

Trevor and Gav watched him and listened to his story, as he practically yelled out the details of the afternoon.

His earlier calm had evaporated and he talked recklessly. Inwardly Trev smiled: in this mood, Ricky was ready for any wild scheme.

'You didn't say that to him!' said Gav, as Ricky heaped accusations on his dad.

'Course not,' snapped Ricky. 'Of course I didn't. I took his feelings into account. Not that they ever did the same for me.'

Gav wanted to say that that wasn't true. He couldn't believe that any parents truly didn't care; he couldn't bear to believe that. 'They must have.'

Trev waited until Ricky had calmed down before he mentioned his own news, letting his decision to leave town slip into the conversation at just the right moment.

Ricky was stunned. 'You're joking, Trev. Not now.... Why?'

Trev shrugged. 'It's been on my mind for ages. And now....' He told Ricky about Charlie Pitts, and that set off another outburst.

'The bloody rat!' shouted Ricky. 'That jealous little git!'

'Yeah, always hated me,' said Trev. 'Still, there'll be a send-off.'

Carefully he suggested the idea of one last break-in, as a kind of farewell.

He needn't have been cautious: Ricky's wildness was commanding him.

'Definitely, Trev – definitely. We've got to do that. The team in action. All of us – we'll convince Mark somehow. I'm up for it. I'll go in first. We'll do the most dangerous let-in we've ever done. I'll take the risks. The team – the only bloody people I can trust....'

Gav felt worried, but he didn't dare show it – not

with Ricky in this mood and Trev encouraging it. *Maybe tomorrow they'll feel different....* Somehow, though, Gav sensed they wouldn't. It was as if the group had gone into self-destruct mode and were determined to hurtle stupidly, recklessly, into any chance of a break-in that came their way.

Eight

The noise of the rain was like a crowd shouting, the individual voices of billions of raindrops calling together. The rain slapped the pavements and rushed the gutters. It threw itself at cars and shelters. It ran like commandos across roofs and down embankments. And in the coldness of night-time it ran amok, unchecked, through gardens and streets, like an invading enemy.

The four lads sheltered in a shop doorway, pressed back from the entrance. Behind them a sign flicked on and off, advertising, in yellow lights, 'Carrogan's De Luxe Golf Bags'. It was an expensive shop, for an exclusive neighbourhood of large, three-storey detached houses in sand-coloured Victorian brick. Their biggest target yet, as Trev had pointed out three days earlier.

For three nights, all night, they'd watched in shifts to see if the couple in 183 would go out. Trev, who'd cased the house, promised they would.

They were youngish, he said, they looked trendy, they liked clubbing till all hours. So far, nothing – which had pleased Mark, who'd been very quiet since Trev had taken over everything. Gav and Ricky were the most impatient for the break-in. Gav wanted to get it done and finished and out of the way forever: the last job, and good riddance. Ricky was still brooding and seething about his father; he hadn't spoken to his mum all week, to avoid a row.

'You're never gonna be able to leave town at this rate, Trev,' sniped Mark, pulling up his coat hood. 'Three bloody days.'

'But it's only rained tonight,' said Trev calmly. 'It'll be tonight.'

Gav shivered in the wet gusts of wind. 'How d'you know?'

'I don't,' said Trev. 'Just a feeling. They're the sort who go out when the weather gets 'em down. Not the type to sit in with their feet up. They'll go out for a wild time.'

Ricky muttered, 'Maybe we should go in anyway.'

'That's madness,' said Gav, taking the suggestion seriously.

'Oh, leave him alone. He's still angry,' Trev said. 'What's the time?'

Mark looked at his old watch. 'Seven-thirty.... What's that? Police car. Get back. Look like we're sheltering.'

'We *are* sheltering,' complained Gav. 'Because it's tipping down.'

Trev shushed them. 'Hold up ... it's not a police car – wrong lights. It's a taxi. One of those Road Wily Company ones. They make them look like cop cars, so they can get through traffic jams and do dodgy short-cuts without getting reported.'

'Where's it stopping?' asked Ricky moodily. He looked grey and unwell, even thinner than usual, and he hadn't been sleeping. He couldn't work out what was going on inside him, and he couldn't snap out of it.

'Near 183,' said Mark, with his old hopefulness. 'What do the people look like, Trev? Not that we can see much tonight.'

'They always wear the same his-and-hers green coats,' said Trev. 'Those fancy country ones – Barbour coats, aren't they?'

Mark looked rapidly around, like a leopard in

undergrowth. 'Here comes someone.... Yes ... yes, it's 183. The one with the hideous lantern, right? Yep, here they come. Little green hoods up. Into the taxi. Bye-bye, darlings.'

'We've gotta get this right,' said Ricky, bitterly and too loudly.

Gav jumped. 'Calm down, mate. You'll get us nicked.'

'Come on,' said Mark, launching himself into the streaming, slashing wildness of the rain, like a man diving into the ocean off the side of a ship. 'One by one, fifteen seconds between us.' He was taking command again, taking over, out of habit. Gav glanced at Trev; but, strangely, he didn't look bothered at all. So Gav dived into the flooding street after Mark.

He hunched over against the storm, his trousers rapidly turning into soaking flaps of material that clung to his legs like seaweed. He splashed after Mark's retreating figure, keeping him in sight but at the right distance. Gav didn't look back – he knew Ricky would be behind him, and Trev would be keeping lookout at the rear; he just concentrated on Mark. Somehow he felt safer with Mark back in charge. He didn't trust Mark in anything, except in his skill at not getting caught – which was more than enough for tonight's business.

Of course there was no one else out and about: the storm was wild, vicious. Mark ducked down a back alley. This had been the service entrance, for tradesmen, when the big Victorian houses had servants and large families living in them. On either side, the giant dark silhouettes of the houses loomed up, forming a steep corridor of bricks up to a frenzied sky. The houses looked sinister and eerie in the darkness and clamour of the tempest. Gav knew he would feel better once they were all securely

125

inside, behind locked doors, with the heating and the TV on. His trainers leaked water and the rain had bitten his fingers with thousands of tiny sharp teeth.

Behind him, he faintly heard Ricky and Trev splashing through the sticky, heavy mud. In front, Mark crouched at one of the tall wooden back gates. Gav saw him put an arm round the post and pull the bolt on the other side – expertly, skilfully. Mark knew what he was doing. The wind was swirling, but Mark slipped in the gate and held it open a crack so the other three could slide wetly through. Minimum fuss, minimum movement.

They were safely in the garden, and the old thrill returned. Huddled in the shelter of the fence, they smiled at one another, their adrenaline buzzing. Even Gav felt that warm sense of triumph and control override his usual nerves, giving him a wicked courage to continue.

Mark crawled close to Trev and whispered, 'Which door? You cased it. How do we get in?'

'Basement,' said Trev. 'It's in an alcove, down some steps. No one can see. And tonight no one's gonna hear.'

The gardens were as grand as the houses: long, wide stretches of land, dotted with greenhouses, sheds, ornamental ponds, shrubs, nooks and crannies of all sorts. It was easy for the four of them to speed up the path to the back of the house, covered by trees and high hedges. These were people who liked their privacy and probably hated their neighbours. Mark wondered, bitterly, how a young couple could afford such a swanky house. He reckoned they must be business gits or financial swindlers of some sort, people who did more illegal things in a morning at work than he'd ever done with all his break-ins; the sods.

Way in the distance, across the sea, sheet lightning

stretched itself across the clouds. They all ignored it –
except Ricky, who thought he saw something – someone?
– on a nearby rooftop. But that couldn't be. It must have
been just a chimney-stack. He whispered to Trev, 'Did
you see something up on the roof?'

'Don't be daft,' said Trev. 'Get a grip. Let's get inside.'

The wind was rising all the time, and the *whoosh* of its
howling and ferreting sounded like a jet taking off. The
four of them had reached the door to the basement; it
was down a flight of steps, which ran with water like the
levels of a rapid. At the bottom, a couple of old-fashioned
metal dustbins stood like soldiers on guard duty. But at
least they were out of sight and there was a little shelter
here.

Mark was back in charge. 'Trev. Open the door. Any
method.'

Trev smiled and took out two plastic library cards,
sellotaped together for extra thickness and strength. 'See,'
he said, 'it's a Yale lock, and 'cause the gap's so wide, all
... we have ... to do ... is this.' He jerked the cards down
the gap in the door until he reached the lock and pushed
its hammer back. The latch wasn't down. 'Very lax of
them,' smiled Trev.

They slipped into the basement, one by one. Gav had
an uneasy feeling about the place; it gave him the heebie-
jeebies. Trev flicked his lighter. The flame didn't reveal
much, but even by its dim light, they could tell the
basement was like a huge underground maze, stacked
with junk and boxes and metal shelves – a mysterious
warehouse of a place, no doubt home to all kinds of vermin,
which smelt of damp and decay and rotting carpets.

The wind blew out Trev's lighter, and the door
slammed shut with a vibrating smash that seemed to rock

every bone in Gav's body. He freaked.

'What was that? What was that?'

A thin hand gripped his shoulder. 'Shut up, Gav,' hissed Ricky. It was the first time he had ever talked to him like that, and Gav felt sad for his friend who was acting so hard and so strange.

Mark went back and tried the door. 'It's jammed. The lock's jammed.'

'No,' whispered Trev. 'One of the dustbins has got jammed up against it. It's the wind. Doesn't matter – there's an upstairs back door, too. We don't need to go out the way we came in.'

Ricky wasn't convinced. 'It's one less escape route if there is any trouble, though, isn't it? I mean, the shape on the roof –'

'What shape?' demanded Trev. 'Has everyone gone mad or something?'

Mark took over. 'Trev's right. Come on; this is his farewell break-in. Look, we're in, the people are out – let's get cooking, right?'

Trev re-lit his lighter to let Ricky find the light switch. When the single shivering bulb was on, they saw the real extent of the cellar. It stretched for yards and yards, clotted with pillars and supporting arches, into a darkened distance of indistinct shapes – piles of stuff and another doorway, probably to a garage. It was impossible to see all of it in the dingy light, but they made out a rickety set of stairs leading up to the ground floor.

'It's gonna be right posh up there,' whispered Mark. 'Only the best tonight, lads.'

In single file, they crept up the stairs, which creaked and moaned like a ship's rigging at every step. Outside, the woollen anger of the storm continued. Mark pushed open the cellar door and stepped into the hallway. *He's brave*, thought Gav, *you have to give him that: he doesn't mind going first*. The others followed him into the main house.

They saw straightaway how magnificent the house must have once been. The space was almost frightening; it seemed like there were doors everywhere, like each door couldn't possibly lead to a separate room. But the decoration was shabby and the paintwork scrappy. The hallway didn't look lived-in.

'I think they've only just moved in,' explained Trev, staring around.

Gav looked around warily. He wanted to stay close to the others: this place was too big. You couldn't feel comfortable in a house like this. Where did you sit? How did you fill up the space with noise and people and furniture and life? He whispered to Ricky, 'It's enormous – like a palace. How could anyone feel comfortable here?'

'Easily,' said Ricky bitterly, looking down the darkened hall.

Outside, the rain and wind kept up their battering. The thick walls smothered the noise; it felt as though they were actually underwater. Inside, the house was alive with distant creaks and moans.

'These old houses are full of noises,' said Trev, trying to calm down Gav, who was nervously glancing up the main staircase.

'You sure there's no one in?' asked Gav.

'Don't be daft,' snapped Mark. 'Why're we standing here? Let's get to the kitchen. Come on, Gav. Don't ruin Trev's last break-in.'

They padded down the hallway towards the kitchen. Ricky went first, his usual need for grub giving him extra impetus. He pulled down the blinds on the kitchen windows and flicked on the fluorescent lights.

'Look at this place,' he breathed. The kitchen was vast, dominated by a large pine rectory table adorned with an overflowing bowl of fruit. 'It's like a magazine. Perfect home photo.'

'Get started,' ordered Mark. 'I'm gonna drop the latch on the front door. Don't want any interruptions, do we?' He started off back down the hallway.

Gav was oddly quiet; he wandered around, tapping the cupboard doors, instead of starting the cooking. 'What's up?' Trev asked him. 'We haven't got all night.'

'I'm thinking about Death-Breath again,' admitted Gav. 'You don't think –'

'No, I don't,' said Trev.

Ricky felt sorry for Trev. It seemed like Gav was determined to ruin his grand farewell. 'I'll get started,' he said, pulling open the fridge door.

Then he froze. A loud metallic clang from outside echoed above the roar of the storm, and a shadow flicked across the window. Gav panicked. 'What was that?'

'Nothing,' said Trev. 'Just the trees. Calm down, you're making me nervous too.... Where's Mark got to?'

They looked silently at one another, listening; they couldn't hear him in the hall.

👁 👁 👁

Mags Lindenfield, the telephone receiver to her ear, raised her eyebrows in surprise to her friend Carla. Carla shrugged.

'Well, it's nice to speak to you,' said Mags. 'I don't think we've ever spoken before, have we? I know my

Gav's a good friend of your Ricky, but they seem to keep their parents a secret.'

Linda laughed. 'Ashamed of us. Secretive devils, the pair of them.... I'm sorry to ring out of the blue, but is Ricky there?' She stopped for a moment. 'He's been acting oddly lately. We've had a little ... a problem in the family that's upset him. I haven't seen much of him. I wouldn't normally ring. I'm not one of those fussy mothers' – she was aware that she sounded just like one – 'the ones who can't let go, you know. I don't see him much, as it is....' What was she saying? Ricky's visit to his dad had upset Linda more than she'd expected. She'd been worried by Ricky's state of mind when he'd come back: he seemed determined to do something – maybe something wild....

'When do we ever?' sympathised Mags. 'Same with Gav – in and out like a cat. I was thinking of getting a flap for him.'

Linda laughed. 'Tell me about it. But lately it's been worse than ever.... And I don't like some of the types Ricky's involved with.' The truth was that this had been building up for some time, and she hadn't known who to talk to about it. Mrs Lindenfield had a reputation for being a calm person, somebody who talked good sense.

'You mean that article Mark.'

'Yes, him. There's something damaged about him. His family ... well, you know.'

'I do know. But your Ricky's not here at the moment. Neither is Gav, actually. Come to think of it, Geoff, my husband, cleared off somewhere too. Men – they're like shadows: slippery, the lot of them.'

'Perhaps I shouldn't worry.' Linda sounded tearful. 'I shouldn't have rung and disturbed you.'

'Don't be silly. You sound upset, dear. Look – why

131

don't you pop round for a drink? If they're together, they might come back here. Besides, now we've met – on the phone, at least – we could swap notes on our lads. That'll surprise the little beggars.'

Linda hesitated. She felt lonely, isolated, and she was anxious for Ricky, who was clearly in a strange mood these days.

'I've just poured myself a nice martini,' persisted Mags. 'D'you know the address? Come on round. I know it's raining, but the company'll do you good.'

Does she know about me? wondered Linda, staring out of her window at the beating rain. *A filthy night – still....*

'I will,' said Linda. 'I will. I could take a taxi.... I'm sorry, but what's your name?'

'Margaret, but everyone calls me Mags.'

'I'm Linda. What a change – using someone's name. I'm right fed up with being thought of as "Ricky's mum". I'd forgotten I've got a name.'

Mags chuckled. 'We've clearly got a lot to chat about.'

'Right,' said Linda. 'I'll be there in ten minutes.'

Mags put down the phone. She didn't feel as jokey as she'd sounded. Where did Gav creep off to all the time? And where was Geoff, out gallivanting on a night like this?

She took another glass out of the cabinet and sliced some extra lemon. 'Well, Carla, let's hope the one bottle'll be enough,' she smiled.

Outside, the rain spat and the wind growled and the world seemed like some untameable beast, clawing at the windows of her home.

Gav thought he heard something but he didn't move. *Something's wrong,* he thought; *I knew it was going to go wrong – I knew it.* Trev put his finger to his lips to shush them and pointed towards the door to indicate that he was going to investigate. Ricky brooded, leaning against the cooker; he didn't seem to care what was going on. Gav sidled over to him as Trev left the kitchen and headed into the large gloom of the hallway.

Quietly, Trev padded along the hallway towards the front door. He kept close to the skirting board, pressing himself to the wall. The hall seemed vast, as long as a hotel corridor. He rounded a corner and crouched behind an ornamental plant in a ceramic stand. From there, he could see the front door.

Two shadowy figures were scuffling on the mat. Mark was wrestling helplessly in the grip of a large man who had one hand over his mouth. Mark's eyes were large and white and scared in the darkness. He was trying to warn Trev; he was trying to pull free, get the hand away and call out.

He twisted and wriggled desperately against the strong arms that imprisoned him, and finally he tore his head away from the restraining grasp.

'Get out, Trev! Police – a trap – get –' Then the hand, hard in a leather glove, clamped itself on his mouth again.

Trev bolted down the hallway, shouting wildly. His ears pulsated to the sound of the storm, Mark's cries and the clatter of feet running from their hiding-places all over the house. 'Get out!' screamed Trev. 'It's a trap!'

He hurtled into the kitchen, where Gav and Ricky had leapt for the back door and were wrenching at the handle. With a splintering smash, the glass of the door caved in and a dark-blue sleeve shot through, scrabbling for the inside lock.

'They're outside!' shouted Gav, panicking. 'We're surrounded!'

The back door shuddered as a hefty shoulder slammed against woodwork, hard enough to knock the whole house down. In the garden a searchlight flicked on, throwing a violent beam of light into the kitchen.

Trev was the calmest. He grabbed Ricky roughly. 'Follow me. Upstairs. Gav, come on. Move yourself, *now*.'

The three lads bundled through the kitchen door, lost their bearings and stumbled into the main living-room. Several shadowy figures sprang out of the bleak darkness. More police. Three of them. Big men, and determined. Ricky dived over a sofa and rolled across the carpet, dodging the men's first lunge. Gav used his speed and ran – first left, then right, like his old rugby moves – and found himself free, near the stereo stack. He pulled it down sideways and had the satisfaction of seeing someone go sprawling on the floor with a crash of expensive electrical equipment. Voices called out, 'Over there! Grab 'em! Get the little sods....'

Ricky felt a strong hand grab his arm. He wriggled and slipped out of the grip, his thinness helping him out. Where was Gav? Where was Trev? Should he help them or try to get away? Anything, anything rather than get caught.... All around him, the thump and smash of furniture and ornaments and books, flying, crashing, breaking and falling, confused his senses. But he knew he wasn't caught – not yet. He wasn't caught yet.

'Gav – Ricky – run for it!' came Trev's voice. 'Get out! I've had it.... Go!'

Ricky glanced into the darkness. He could see Trev

134

struggling in a bear hug, and a plainclothes copper gripping his waist and nearly hefting him off the ground. Trev was lost – the man who had him was obviously a maniac. Ricky didn't know DS George Tate, but he'd judged his character right and true after only a two-second glance: George Tate wasn't a man to let go once he'd closed his grip on a victim.

It was happening so fast that no one had time to go for a light switch. The blackened house increased the confusion and gave Ricky at least some cover; he dodged round an armchair and out of the living-room. He knew the front and back doors would be covered, but had the police thought about the cellar? He bounded down the hall. There was his answer: a burly shape guarded the cellar door. Ricky ran for the stairs, where he collided with Gav dashing out of the living-room. They were fitter and faster than their pursuers.

'Gav – quick – the stairs! Follow me.' And Ricky dragged Gav up the first flight.

Mark's strained voice followed them. 'No! You'll be trapped!' Then there was the unmistakeable smack of a punch to the jaw, and he went quiet.

Gav and Ricky reached the first landing at breakneck speed. It was hopeless, they knew. There were plenty of places to hide, rooms going off in all directions, but it would only be a matter of time before they were found. But Ricky didn't care about that – he wanted to stay free as long as he could – and Gav was so scared he just followed his friend.

'Keep going, Gav,' urged Ricky. 'Up to the next floor. They're not coming after us yet – don't know why.'

The reason why was that the police team downstairs knew they had them cornered and were making sure of

Mark and Trev. Mark was finally handcuffed at the front door, while Trev was dragged into the kitchen by DS Tate.

'I've got this one. Go after the other two,' he ordered his spare officers.

Trev saw a chance and wrenched free, lunging for the dish-rack and flinging it at Tate. Tate fell against the sink, giving Trev just enough time to open the back door and dive out. The storm broke into the house in a howl of rain and wind. Tate recovered and lurched after Trev, bawling, 'I'll get him – go for the others!'

Despite the wild slashing rain, Tate picked out the fleeing shape of Trev, dodging down the huge garden and ploughing into the cover of the main shrubs. Tate had studied a plan of the garden and memorised its layout; he set off after him, taking the left-hand path – a short-cut.

Trev, crouching low, had slunk behind the shed, between the fence and the compost incinerator, deep in dark shadows. He tried to hold his breath. It seemed as if his gasps could be heard above the roar of the storm. He tuned in his ears, trying to pick out the sound of footsteps. There, to the right, coming slowly, deliberately: DS Tate pushing aside undergrowth. A relentless man who never gave up.

Trev took a breath. 'Over here,' he hissed. 'I'm over here.'

Tate changed direction and found himself face to face with Trevor.

'Well, you made it look good,' he said.

'I had to,' answered Trev steadily. 'D'you think Mark'd rest until he evened the score, if he knew it was me?'

Tate took an envelope out of his pocket and turned it

in his hand. 'So Mark's the leader? And we've got him. Here's your money.'

He handed the envelope to Trev. 'Remember the deal, Trevor. You take this and you get out of my town for good. Come back and I'll do you for every offence I can make stick.'

Trev shrugged. He had the money he needed to start afresh elsewhere. He wouldn't be coming back.

'I don't suppose your friends'll want to see you again, either,' said Tate. 'Nobody likes a grass, not even me. I suppose that article Ernie down the park'll get the blame, won't he? Not that you care. That's how you planned it, didn't you? Make it look like he was the grass all along. Very clever. But one day, young man, you might learn there's more to things than just looking out for yourself. Now get out.'

Without hesitation, Trev turned, leapt the fence and disappeared across the gardens, heading straight for the bus station. He didn't trust Tate any more than Tate respected him.

Tate rushed back to the house and bounded up to the first landing, where his officers were systematically searching the rooms.

'What you doing?' he bellowed. 'They'll have gone up. Get after them.'

Two flights up, Gav and Ricky steeled themselves for the inevitable. Up here there were only small attic rooms, nowhere to hide. Gav whispered, 'We're not gonna fight them, are we, Ricky?'

'Don't be daft. That'd be asking for trouble. Listen, Gav. You've got to think straight, right? They've only caught us in here. They can't touch us for the other places. So don't fall to bits and start confessing, yeah?'

137

Gav nodded. Where had Ricky found this new toughness all of a sudden?

'They're coming,' hissed Ricky. 'This is it.'

Two flights below, the officers started slowly up the stairs. DS Tate's voice called, 'Right, lads – you up there! We don't want any fuss, do we? No heroics. You're trapped. You can't get away. You might as well come down nice and quiet.'

Gav found himself blurting out, 'Yes – I'm coming down....'

Ricky smiled: *Let them wait.* 'Shame we haven't got a hang-glider, mate.'

But Gav wasn't listening. He was staring up at the low ceiling, dumbstruck. Directly above them, the loft door had opened, and a face was peering down. It was Gav's dad and he was holding out his hand.

'Dad? But –'

'Shh. Grab my hand,' whispered Geoff. 'Then you, Ricky.'

He hoisted the two lads effortlessly into the loft and quickly, silently, replaced and locked the door. They were in darkness again.

Nine

The three of them stared at one another in silence while the storm boomed and clattered against the roof outside, echoing round the loft space with a sinister fury. Geoff had his finger on his lips and an urgent look in his eyes.

As their eyes got used to the darkness, Gav and Ricky realised there was some light slipping in through a window set in the roof. Geoff pointed towards it. It was their only means of escape.

'Quietly,' whispered Geoff. He looked relieved, but Gav recognised the hidden anger in the tense jawline. *Who would be worse: Dad or the police?*

They followed Geoff to the window. Their feet seemed to crash on the loft flooring like concrete blocks. Down below, they heard the first officers arrive at the top landing and dart into the attic rooms.

'Come on,' hissed Geoff, opening the window. The full power of the storm hit them in cold blasts of rain and wind.

'It's too dangerous,' said Gav.

'Shh,' said Geoff. 'It's two paces to a flat section of roof. Just step out. Two steps. You can't fall. There's another section juts out just below us....'

He hoisted Gav through the window. Outside, the gale ripped at Gav's coat and grabbed his legs, but he saw that the flat roof was as close as his dad had said, and he stepped onto it. It was bounded by a railing that led to an old-fashioned fire escape.

'You next,' said Geoff, and hoisted Ricky out. He came last, and as he climbed out he heard a shout below. The

139

police had heard the noise in the loft and guessed what was happening.

'They're on the roof!' screamed Tate's voice. 'Get downstairs and get on the radio to the car outside!'

Geoff leapt to the fire escape. But even if the three of them could make it down before the police got there, where would they go then? He found he was excited, not scared; he'd been a wild young man himself, twenty-five years before.

He grabbed Gav by the jacket and took Ricky's arm. The wind swirled around them; their hair was already sopping wet, their trousers and shoes soaked. 'Back in!' bawled Geoff. He practically slung them through the window and climbed nimbly in himself. He was used to clambering about on roofs.

'We've got to get to the cellar,' he hissed, 'while they're occupied outside. It's a gamble. Come on.'

He lifted the loft door and dropped silently onto the carpet of the attic room. Gav and Ricky followed. They pattered down the stairs, which were frighteningly well-lit now; no cover, no hiding-places. They reached the ground floor in seconds and headed for the cellar.

The constable on guard had gone; Tate had pulled everyone outside, to the fire escape. The three of them had just time to get through the cellar door and bolt it before they heard the officers' bewildered cries echoing outside and the clatter of boots running down the side alley.

Geoff went down the steps but didn't head for the back cellar door: he'd seen the police block it off earlier, from his vantage point on the roof. Ricky had half-spotted him from the garden; but the police had never even thought of looking up at the roof.

'Dad. We're trapped,' said Gav. 'What're we doing down here?'

'Be quiet,' ordered Geoff. 'Leave it to me.' He wove around the boxes to the front of the cellar and scrabbled about in a corner, muttering to himself. Then they heard his voice: 'Over here.'

When they joined him, he was kneeling beside a low wooden door, levering it open with the screwdriver he always carried.

'What is it?' asked Ricky.

'External coal-hole,' said Geoff. 'Don't you know your architecture? I've been a builder in this town for twenty years.' He wrenched the door open and crouched through the low archway. It was pitch-black and stank of damp and urine. Gav and Ricky reluctantly followed.

'Now we've got to get lucky,' whispered Geoff. 'Hope they're all round the back. This manhole, up here ... I can just feel it ... it should take us out to the end of the front garden.' He turned to where he thought his son was. 'Gav? Were there bushes in the front garden?'

Ricky answered instead; he was the observant one. 'Yes ... Mr Lindenfield.'

'Right. Here goes, then.' Geoff lifted the hidden coalhole lid, pushing against the weight of stray earth and stones. Straining every muscle, he slid it to one side. A funnel of cold air rushed through the opening, sucking the furious sound of the storm down with it.

Geoff twisted and strained to get his broad shoulders through the narrow opening. Luckily, the Victorian design meant he could just make it. He popped out into a thick covering of shrubs and helped the lads out behind him. But they still weren't safe. They'd only made it into the front garden.

Behind them, the house was fully lit and vibrating with the shouts and stamps of the searching police officers. Out in the street, the blue flashes of light from the squad cars had no doubt attracted onlookers. There had to be other policemen at the parade of shops that lined the best escape route, and there were probably more on their way. To Ricky, the situation seemed hopeless; he was almost resigned to being caught. But Geoff didn't panic. Gav was amazed at his father's cunning and quick thinking. He realised his dad was risking his reputation, his business, his good name to help him. But Geoff's face suggested this was no time for compliments or thanks.

Geoff parted the bushes and surveyed the scene in the road. It wasn't too bad: only one police car, and an unmarked car on the other side of the street. It was a small operation, then. He smiled to himself: hardly high-priority.

Because of the venom of the storm, nobody had come out to see the fun. Most of the neighbours contented themselves with peering out from their rain-splashed windows. At the kerb, a solitary uniformed officer kept watch over Mark, who was handcuffed and locked in the car. The gate was guarded; but, with a slight diversion, they might make it over the fence at the opposite side of the garden.

Suddenly another siren sounded, and an ambulance raced along the road and braked outside the house. The three watchers in the bushes didn't know it, but one of the officers on the fire escape had injured his leg. The paramedics leapt out of the ambulance and unloaded a stretcher.

'You two,' hissed Geoff, 'get ready. Here's our chance.'

While the officer on the kerb directed the paramedics down the path, Geoff, Gav and Ricky wriggled along the line of shrubs and slid over the fence, across an alleyway and into the neighbouring garden.

From there, it was easy. They crossed three or four more gardens before they slipped out onto the pavement and disappeared down a side street. They were safe; they'd got away.

Geoff made them separate and told the boys to meet him back at home. 'Take different routes, and don't hurry – don't run. Keep to the side alleys.' He stared at Gav. 'Get back safely. I want a few words with you.'

The street-lights passed by on either side of him, blurred by the speed of the car and the lashing rain; the seats smelt of cleaning fluid; the constables sat with their wet uniforms steaming slightly. Mark gazed straight ahead, feeling the thick unyielding steel of the handcuffs bite his wrists like metal mouths. He was calm; he was inside himself. One day, he realised, he'd known he'd be caught one day. What could they do? Beat him like his dad always had? Insult him like his mum had? The policemen were nothing. The 'home' they'd give him couldn't be worse than his usual one. And his friends....

Mark smiled. His friends had got away. They were safe. And they'd stay safe: nobody would get their names from him. He was pleased they'd escaped. Who could tell – maybe they'd be a team again someday....

His companions in the police car sat in silence. He knew that they'd failed, and that the maniac who led them was furiously following in his unmarked car, probably dreaming up threats for when they reached the station. *They're in as much trouble as me*, thought Mark, pleased.

He knew he'd been set up; and he knew who it must have been. That grass, that loner from the park – Ernie. When the car drove down a slipway into the guarded car park behind the police station and drew up at the rear entrance to the cells, Mark tensed a little, but he refused to show any fear. But when the two coppers in front got out of the car, opened the boot and took out two green waterproof jackets, he realised the truth.

Those were the coats the couple at 183 had worn when they'd left the house earlier. So that was why the hoods had been up. This meant the police had set a trap; it meant the police had known they were coming. And there was only one way they could have known. Someone had told them.

More than that: someone had chosen that house, made sure it was the target. Someone had betrayed them. And that someone had been Trevor.

When the front door opened, then slammed, the three women flinched. Mags gripped her martini and took another sip, raising her eyebrows to Linda, who was deep in a comfortable armchair.

'That sounds like Geoff. Only two more to go,' she said.

Geoff shook his sopping coat in the hallway and levered off his wet shoes, grunting and muttering like a drunkard. He suddenly bellowed, 'Gavin! Ricky! You back?'

Coming into the living-room, he was surprised to see three women there but sensible enough not to ask questions. 'You called Gav and Ricky,' said Mags. 'Have you seen them? Should they be here, then?'

'Yes, and yes. If they're not here, they will be.' Geoff took his socks off and flung them anywhere.

'Geoff, don't do that. I've got guests,' complained Mags.

Geoff halted. 'Oops. Sorry, ladies – things on my mind. Pardon my bare feet.'

He headed for the kitchen and took out his vodka bottle, which was keeping cool in the fridge. He didn't like to admit it to himself, but he felt a little shaky – him, of all people. He'd done his best – his duty to his son, as he saw it. But he felt guilty, too. He respected the law. Only the thought of that bitter fanatic DS Tate soothed his conscience. Tate didn't care about justice; Tate didn't care about anything. *I know his sort*, Geoff thought.

Mags's voice drifted into the kitchen. 'Geoff? This is Linda – Ricky's mum. She's worried. Geoff, can you come here, please?'

'Coming,' he called, pouring a maximum-size drink. *Getting old*, he thought; *me heart's still pounding.... Must get fitter.*

He went back out to the living-room. 'Is Ricky all right?' asked Linda anxiously. 'He's been odd for days.'

'He's fine, I think,' said Geoff cautiously. 'He'll be back soon, believe me.'

☯ ☯ ☯

Trevor took the night bus from the coach station, but he'd only bought a ticket to the next town. He reckoned Tate had alerted the railway police to pick him up when he arrived at the train station. Trev's plan was to catch a train, but five stops up the line, not here. He wasn't going to leave an easy trail. Tate might check at the bus station and be surprised that Trev had only travelled twenty miles north; but by then Trev would be miles away, on a fast train, bound for the West Country and a temporary place at his cousin's.

As the bus jolted him up and down, Trev put aside any guilt. You had to look after yourself nowadays. Friends – real friends – were a false luxury. So what if he was a user? If he didn't use, he'd be used himself. They should've seen through him. And what would happen to them? Not much. Nothing as bad as being homeless and helpless, the way he had been. They had families to back them up; he didn't.

There was a girl further up the coach. She had a couple of travelling bags with her, and she looked lonely. He might go and chat with her later, make contact. She reminded him of someone ... Zoë. She reminded him of Zoë.

But Zoë was the past. Zoë was gone. And he had himself to look after once again....

The back door clicked open. Gav had made it back, wet and subdued; his eyes were dark and tense. He felt like a criminal, and he was steeling himself for his dad's reaction, which was likely to be pretty extreme. Gav still didn't know if he was really safe or not, and that made him nervous. To top it all, he felt stupid for being in this position. And the thought of having to confess to his mum ... that made him miserable.

'Gavin?' came Geoff's voice from the sitting-room. 'Upstairs, now.'

The tone meant no argument. Gav scrambled up the staircase. As he went, he heard his father talking to Mum and someone else: 'It'll be all right, Mags, love. Let it be. I'll sort it out. You enjoy your martinis. Linda, when Ricky comes back – I know he's your boy, but can I have a few words with him? Thank you. It's important.' Geoff sighed. 'Looks like I might have to give both of them some work....'

Upstairs, Gav didn't exactly hide in his room, although he wished he were somewhere else. He waited for the angry Mad Dad hurricane to arrive.

When Geoff came into the room, all Gav could say was, 'Thanks, Dad – I mean it.... Sorry for the – the – you know.... It –'

'"Sorry for the, you know, it...."' repeated Geoff flatly. 'Yes. Very touching. Cheaper than solicitors, isn't it? Better than the nick.'

Gav coughed ashamed. 'Yes.'

'I'm surprised we're not all in the nick right now. That's only luck, Gavin. Bald luck.'

'I know,' said Gav. 'I hope Ricky's all right. He's not back.'

Geoff snorted. 'He'll be fine. He's thin enough to hide up a drainpipe. You stick out, though – our family always have. I made you out straightaway from the roof tonight, storm or no storm.'

Gav hesitated. 'Dad? How did you know – about the break-ins? When? I don't understand....'

'That's my fault,' said Geoff, sitting on a chair. 'I should've bloody well made sure you understood. Nobody's life's completely secret, Gav – not at your age, at least. I guessed when that bloke committed suicide. I saw the four of you legging it across the garden – I thought it was you, but I couldn't be sure. The bulky one got his coat caught scrambling over the wall. I said to meself –

that can't be our Gav, it can't....'

Gav wondered if his dad had dared to believe it – believe that of the son he put down as too lazy to get out of bed on time.

'It was sneaky, all right. But I checked your coat the next day. It was ripped to pieces at the pocket, where you got stuck on the wall. I saw all that. But I kept my mouth shut. Maybe I should've tackled you about it. Maybe....'

Gav didn't want to sound resentful, but he felt he might have been saved earlier. He hid his embarrassment. 'Why didn't you do nothing, Dad?'

There was hurt in Geoff's eyes. 'I really thought – thought you'd stop. I thought you'd see sense after that. I should've stopped you; I should've told your mother. She'd have stopped you. God, she'd have tied you to a chair to stop you. But I kept it a secret.' He stared at his son. 'And you'll keep it a secret now. And that goes for Ricky, too: say nothing. No one will ever know – except if your mate Mark talks. He's the only one the police got, I heard.'

'He won't,' said Gav, almost tearfully. 'He wouldn't do that.'

Geoff smiled ironically. 'Oh, yeah. All your friends can be trusted, eh? But not your parents. You've got some learning to do, Gav, you have.' He got up and went to the window. 'Your mate Ricky's in the garden.'

'How can you see him?' said Gav. 'He's the best at staying hidden.'

'I've been looking down from roofs all me life, mate. I could see a dropped button, me.' Geoff sighed. 'You lot – you weren't born till the sun came out. How could I see him?'

He laughed, but only for a moment. 'I should've

stepped in. I wanted you to work it out for yourself. I got it wrong.' Then he smiled. 'Don't look so smug, Gavin. I might have been wrong, but not as wrong as you.'

He stopped. Someone was knocking at the front door.

'Might be the police,' said Geoff grimly. 'If it is, you've been in here all night. Wait up – your clothes are wet. Get into some dry togs, quick.'

But it was Ricky, bedraggled and soaked, his thin face pinched by sadness. His cheeks looked hollow and his eyes haunted. Mags sent him straight upstairs, and Gav listened as the reluctant footsteps approached.

When Ricky came quietly into the room, Gav tried to signal to him that things weren't too bad, that Geoff didn't look like he was going to explode in the stress to end all stresses. Geoff was still by the window, holding his glass of vodka, one hand in his pocket and one ear out for any more knocks on the door. He didn't look severe; he looked practical.

He said, 'So you got back all right, Ricky? Anybody stop you or anything?'

Ricky shook his head. 'No, Mr Lindenfield. I took the alleyways.'

'He's good at that,' put in Gav, trying to please his dad.

'I'm sure,' said Geoff. 'You've both been pretty good at sneaking about.'

Ricky unzipped his coat and sat down beside Gav. He still wasn't sure what was coming next, or how safe he was with Mr Lindenfield.

'Um – Dad?' tried Gav hopefully.

'Don't,' said Geoff. 'Don't. Sit quiet and stew.'

The room was quiet. Outside, the rain bored holes in the ground and muddied up the earth, and the wind laughed wildly, like a crazy clown. The curtains fluttered as an invisible draught sniffed its way into the house.

Geoff turned from the window. 'It's not for me to tell you how to go on – though I bloody well should, looking at what a mess you've made. But you got me involved, too. I'm not proud of what I did tonight. I had to do it, for you, Gav; but it wasn't right. You put me in a position I didn't want to be in.'

'We wouldn't expect it next time,' said Ricky, not meaning to sound rude but coming across as cheeky. He winced at his own clumsiness and tensed at Gav's ferocious look, which said: *My dad saved us and you're giving him cheek – watch it, mate.*

'There won't be a next time. I've done my duty; next time, Gav, you take the consequences. Understand? You broke the law – God, I did too. And we were lucky – believe you me – to get away with it.'

He picked up his glass. 'I need another drink.... I'm gonna forget this ever happened. But you two had better get yourselves together, change into dry clothes, in case – in case.... When you're changed, come down and get yourselves a beer from the fridge. Ricky, your mother's in the front room. Surprised? If I was you, I'd think about an apology.'

Ricky nodded, not looking at him.

'Looks like everything turned out satisfactory,' said Geoff dryly. 'Remember, you two: not a word. Never. Tonight never happened.'

Then he looked serious. 'Your mate, that Mark, got caught.'

'He'll say nothing,' said Gav, a tremble in his voice.

'More than I can say for the other one,' said Geoff grimly.

'Who? Trev?'

'Think on it, Gavin,' said Geoff. 'You were set up tonight, sweet as a pudding. Someone did you up. Practically entrapment.'

He left the room. Gav didn't feel like speaking, so he looked out some dry clothes for Ricky, who was sitting miserably on the bed. The room was warm and comfortable, despite the cruel storm still raging outside. *This,* thought Ricky, *is a home. Why did Gav do the break-ins? He didn't need to at all.*

His thoughts must have transmitted themselves to Gav, who collected the clothes grumpily. 'Your mum's downstairs, then,' he said. 'I'm sorry, Ricky, mate.' He was sorry – sorry for Ricky, sorry for Geoff, and sorry for himself for being stupid enough to follow Mark.

'What about?' asked Ricky.

'Your dad and that,' said Gav. 'You being angry and everything – you know.'

'What you talking about? We'd better get changed, hadn't we?' He didn't want to talk about it.

Gav shouted, 'Don't be like that! You know what I meant.'

'Oh, yeah. I do. It's my fault all of a sudden, for being angry with my dad. Blame Ricky for everything.'

'Well, you were annoyed,' said Gav. 'You wanted to do it most.'

'I did not.' But then Ricky went quiet. 'Yeah, I did....' He looked almost tearful. 'Why did Trev? I mean, he–'

Gav backed away from the subject. 'We'd better change. Come on. I'm sort of glad it's over. I didn't realise how much strain the whole thing was.'

'So much for excitement,' said Ricky, finally taking off his coat.

Laughter swept up the stairs. The adults were having a laugh, at least.

'Will it – ?' began Gav. 'Will it seem better tomorrow, Ricky?'

'I expect so.' Ricky didn't look sure. 'Course it will. Yeah.' He suddenly wanted to be home, in his room, staring out the window. Alone.

Gav changed quickly, thinking about the beer in the fridge and how it might take the edge off his nerves. He didn't like keeping secrets from his mum; he'd never felt comfortable doing that. It was right strange, having a secret with Dad – although he was starting to realise that Dad had many secrets that nobody would ever know about. He slipped on his tracksuit.

'See you downstairs, mate. Don't worry. Dad's sorted it out.'

After Gav had gone, Ricky muttered to himself, 'Has he? For who?'

Ricky couldn't help thinking about the others, about everyone who'd been involved in the events of the night. What about Mark?

Alone, without friends, taking the full blame; probably in some cell at the cop shop, possibly afraid – no, he wouldn't be afraid. And what about Trev? Trev, the grass, who'd practically got them all caught. Why? Trev wasn't like that. Ricky wanted to be generous, find reasons and excuses.

Perhaps Trev had had no choice.... There was so much to wonder about beyond the dull fact of not getting caught. Gav, Ricky felt, didn't understand this.

He dressed and started down the stairs, breathing deeply, trying to feel calm. Mum? What was she doing here? Nothing was simple; nothing was straightforward.

He entered the front room. His mum jumped up. 'Ricky, what's going on? I've been out of my mind with....'

👀 👀 👀

Ricky sat in his bedroom with a piece of paper and a pen. He realised it had been nearly a year since he'd actually written anything down. In all that time, not a letter, a word, a diary entry – not even a note to his mum. How come he'd forgotten about pens and paper? It felt reassuring, suddenly, to have the pad on his lap and the magic stick in his hand.

'I'm gonna work a few things out,' he muttered.

He wrote 'NOW' at the top of the paper and 'THEN' at the bottom. Where was he now, and where did he want to be in a year's time? He put down some headings – 'WORK', 'DAD', 'LOVE', 'HOME', 'FUN' – but there wasn't much to put under them. Down on paper, his life looked pretty empty.

For half an hour, he stared at the blank sheet and daydreamed. Finally he put under 'DAD': 'I've finally seen him now. Time to think more about Mum.' That was that column finished. Under 'WORK', he listed all sorts of jobs he might like to do – some impossible, some fanciful: he didn't have the qualifications, the connections or the know-how. Most of his choices meant years of training, and when he listed the steps he'd have to take to be ready for each job, it was depressing. He wanted too much, too early. 'FUN' was another washout: there wasn't fun without cash – not in this town. Maybe not anywhere.

He put down the pen in despair. He felt lost, stranded in a desert. He wasn't used to feeling hopeless. At least the break-ins had given him a kind of purpose.

Looking round his bedroom, he noticed some books on the shelf by the bed, antiques left over from the time when he used to read a lot and enjoy it. How he'd hated that last year at school. It had driven him away from books. Most of the time, he'd bunked off with his mates.

Was it, though ... was it still possible to go to college? Get on a course and do some re-sits? Others had done it. His teachers had always said he was bright but lazy. Slowly, he wrote down the word 'COLLEGE'.

It sat there – the word – like a magic sign. Yes. Yes, it would be a breathing space in which to think. New friends, maybe. Love? Except for Trev (where was he now?) they hadn't mixed much with girls. They'd become a silly secret club. But college ... it seemed to draw the other headings together.

Suddenly the idea excited him. It wouldn't be like school; and it had a purpose, and a social life. Mum would be happier. He might contact Dad, to ask him to pay for travel and books and suchlike. If there was money waiting for him, that money Dad said he'd put aside, why not use some of it now?

Ricky felt sure Mum could talk to Dad on the phone about that. Quickly, he sketched out a plan of action – who he had to contact, who to ring, where he might go. Even as he did it, he felt his mind opening up and his heart expanding. Why had he been holding himself back for so long?

He got up and looked out over the darkened gardens, the scene he loved so much. He'd been stuck in some night-time garden in his mind for too long. He needed daylight again. And tomorrow he'd make his first call. He'd make it happen. There were whole new areas to break into – a whole new world to challenge him.

Ten

The two figures had worked their way down the garden in the darkness, avoiding any patches of light and using the bushes for cover. It was a big garden, in an area of large, expensive houses. Garth and Steve were confident they hadn't been seen, and equally confident that the owner of the house was out. Rumour said he was rich and liked to fill his home with expensive items.

In this digital age, there was more to thieving than forcing doors. Steve reckoned he could bypass any electronic security system – even this one, which was state-of-the-art stuff. Good – he liked a challenge. On his back, he had a small bag of tools and gizmos. The physical side of things he left to Garth. They were a strong team.

They reached the back entrance and knelt down by the power-box hidden near the pipes.

'Can you neutralise it?' whispered Garth.

'No problem,' said Steve. 'Every system has a weakness.'

'And,' said a strange voice behind them, 'so does every plan.'

A young man stepped out of the shadows. He was slim and fit, with a moustache and a smart suit; he was smoking a cigarette, and he had a powerful aura of success, of complete, fearless confidence.

'Don't bother running,' he said, and his voice held the two lads in their places. 'Besides, I'm not going to call the police. So you could neutralise the system, could you? That's a dummy box there, a decoy. What about the back-up system?'

'Double bluff,' said Steve. 'The dummy box is really the first system; and the back-up's vulnerable to certain frequencies. I've got a jammer in my bag.'

'Really?' said the man. 'There's no jammer on the market yet.'

'Made it myself,' said Steve warily.

'Thought so,' said the man. 'Couple of clever ones, eh?'

Garth, though he was scared of this self-assured stranger, was bursting to ask a question. 'How did you spot us? We've never been caught before.'

The man smiled. 'It's my business.' He took out a card and handed it to Garth. It read: 'Trevor Holland Security Consultants Ltd.'

Trev put out his cigarette. 'Now then,' he said briskly, 'you seem to have a choice. When you leave here, as you're going to in a few minutes, you either lie low for a bit until you can't help yourselves planning another job – you'll keep going until you're caught; it's bound to happen – or you come round to see me tomorrow and let me see that jammer so my technicians can assess its viability. It's a straight offer, lads. I've been on both sides of this business.' He pointed to his magnificent house. 'Guess which side brings the most rewards.'

'Serious?' asked Steve, noting a ruthless glint in the stranger's eyes.

Trev nodded. 'Yep. One day, if you carry on like this, you'll end up doing something you regret. Doing someone wrong to keep your own freedom. Believe me, I know. Then you'll spend a lot of time making up for it.' He stopped; he'd said too much. 'Now clear off, the pair of you. Go the way you came.'

The two lads took his cue and legged it down the

garden. Trev watched them go and lit another cigarette. He envied them their friendship. Nowadays, it seemed he didn't have anyone he could sincerely call a friend.

👁 👁 👁

Gav looked around nervously and took a large swig from his pint. He glanced at Ricky and whispered, 'Are they all intellectuals here, mate?'

Ricky laughed. 'Think they are. You've got big, Gav.'

'Yep.' Gav flexed a powerful arm. 'It's the work. On the sites.' He was broad and strong, tanned from working outdoors. His hands were muscular and hard. 'You're as skinny as ever.' He shook his head. 'So you're a doctor now. Can't believe it.'

'PhD,' corrected Ricky. 'Doctor of Literature and Poetry. Did you like the ceremony?'

'Best thing you ever did, going back to college,' Gav said. He had come up to Kent University to see Ricky receive his doctorate, and he felt nervous in this company of students and professors and lecturers. 'You always had brains. Another drink?'

'Yeah. Cheers.'

'Not much money in it, though.' Gav laughed: he was well off now, in his new house, recently married to Louise.

'Your mum looked well, this afternoon,' he said, as he came back from the bar. 'Shame she had to get going.'

'Linda? Yeah.'

'You call her Linda now, eh? Well trendy. My mum won't stand for anything but Mum. She says she's earned it.' Gav grinned. 'Still, I'm glad she's happy with that new fella, your mum – I mean Linda. She's a looker still.'

'You sound like –' Ricky broke off. 'Forget it.'

Gav rather shyly rummaged in his bag and took out a book. On the back was Ricky's photo.

'Ricky, mate – sign this for me. It's your book of poems. Got it as soon as it came out.'

'I know what it is,' said Ricky. 'What'd you buy one for? I was going to give you one anyway.'

Gav put up his hand. 'Oh no, had to buy it. Pay my way, me. The more you sell, the quicker you'll break in....' He faltered. 'To the big time.'

'Break in,' muttered Ricky, and the pair of them stared silently at each other, sharing those images from the past: Death-Breath, the night of the storm, Trev's betrayal, Mark....

'How's your dad?' asked Ricky.

'Same as ever,' said Gav. 'Works less now. Leaves more and more of the running up to me. He's the senior partner, he says, which leaves me – don't it? – as the working partner.' Gav took back the book of poems and opened it. 'Read some of these last night. Can't pretend I could make any sense of most of 'em – I mean, what must go on in your head, mate.... But this one here – now, that was a different story; this one about the window and looking out at the gardens at night. I liked that. Brought back memories, it did. You got the atmosphere of those nights spot on.'

He looked at Ricky. 'I'm glad we stayed mates, Ricky. And I'm glad you didn't get poncy 'cause of your brains.'

'Who else is gonna buy me beer?' smiled Ricky.

'Not this lot,' laughed Gav, glancing around. 'And someone needs to give 'em advice about clothes – I mean, look at them....'

Ricky sipped his beer. 'Fancy a game of darts?'

'Yeah, why not? Wait up; no money, though. Some

things don't change – like your throwing arm.... Ricky? What d'you think happened to Mark? He never came back to town, when he got out.'

'I don't know,' said Ricky. 'He didn't have much to come back to.'

They looked at each other. They both hoped Mark had found the home he'd longed for so much, somewhere ... anywhere.

👁 👁 👁

The hard-faced young man concentrated as he split the packet of birdseed and tipped it, through a cupped hand, into the metal cartridges. He capped them and loaded them into the shotgun. He cocked the gun, then uncocked it and opened the barrels before giving it to a younger lad sitting across the table.

'Why birdseed, Mark? What for?' asked the lad.

'Don't be stupid,' said Mark. 'You fire it into the ceiling of the bank when we arrive. Straight upwards. Hell of a mess. Takes half the polystyrene off the ceiling, scares the staff, scares the fat stuffing out of the customers; but if we get caught – and we won't – we can't get done for firearm violence.' He looked angry, but he said coolly, 'Break in, get out, get away. Don't argue. Just follow the plan. Follow the plan, and we're away. The guard we're about to do knows that. But I've got his measure, moustache or no. He'll recognise me when we come through the front door, all right.'

The lad nodded. He wanted the excitement of a bank raid, and the power, but he didn't want to get nicked; and this Mark had never been nicked for a raid. The way he planned, how could he be?

Mark turned to another lad sitting across the room and said, 'Go and test the car again.'

'I've done it five times already.'

'Do it six.'

'Why?' asked the lad.

'Breaking in's the easy bit. Breaking out's always been the hardest part.'